Yolo

The Lovely Little Lunatic

Sa'id Salaam

Yolo

Dedications

First and foremost I want to praise and thank my Lord for absolutely everything. It's not possible to count His favors and blessings, so I won't even try. Instead I thank Him for everything.

Next, the ladies of my life: my wife Jennah, Mom Diedra, Grandma Rainey, daughters Bryonna and Jessica, and my granddaughters Aliya and Liv.

My man's and dem: my sons, grandson, brothers, cousins and err body else.

Acknowledgments

And of course all of y'all, the readers.... Athea Cranford, Ghoul Field, LaKeysa, Shine, Diana S., Cassandra Hayes, Myijai, Karen Taylor, Tammy Powell Herbert, Toshiba, Shanika, Denise Miller, Love, cssmlf@yahoo.com, Miss Keshia Henry, Byron Mathis, Rosie, Damion Hamilton, Tanisha Barrett, Tisha Wills, Lakeshia, Rhonda, Malisha Marie Jones, Saima Mann, Gwendolyn Allen Lawson G Law, Laurie Starr Thomas, Patryce Johnson, Clarice MsRere Henry, Chef Brooklyn Shandy, Amie, Aisha Berry, Kastin Blak, Missy Yel, Stacey Michelle Hunt, Cynt Lil Cuba Lady Aces SC prez, CeCe Lucas, Marcel Ford, Tanisha Reed, Karimah, Tee Tee Aintworriedaboutdanext Samuels, Stacey Nelson, LaVina Richardson, Betty Imthatdamngood Bethea, Antoinette Mitchell Tate, Imanni Bella Angel Gaye, Rebecca Ortiz, Areya Square, Krystal Johnson, Rashida, Sarah Clowers, Tasha Williams, Helena Harris, Niecy Niece Tyson, LaShawn Green, Lissha, Iona Sawyer, Jerrice Owens, Troi Thompson, Anissa, Shandi obsessedwithpurple Guibeaux, Liltinybk Williams Liltinybk Williams, Neice Sanders, Tammy Jernigan, Author Sunshine, Felicia Coleman Brown, Yolanda Evans Harris, Benita Williams, Lera Murray, Enez Welch, Dion E Cheese@iurban.org, Denise Moore, Sylina Freeman, Stephanie Thompson, Natasha Potts, Kim Fonda, Tonya Everett, Kateri Young, Lisa Bryant, LaShonna Tinner Gross, Bernie Bagley, Anita Guerra, Yolanda R. Ray, Sharon

LadyShay, Jacque (JJ) Jones, Patricia Watkins, NeKesha Milton, Kimberly Carter, Michelle Wilson, Latonya LadyBlaize Knight, Kayla MeBendez, AbdulHaqq, Meaka Imperfectbeauty Garner, Vanessa Speaks, Tamisha Daunyale Scruggs, Kathleen Lucas, Priscilla Murray, Pista Pete, Monique Colter, Alicia Jel-lo Dean, Cheryl Kitchen Lewis, Lisa Saxon, and Bree. Thanks for all of your loyal support, encouragement, suggestions, and love. Team Salaam!!!!

Prologue

"Damn it Philomina, did you have to put these so tight!" Thadeous Frank grumbled straining once more to free himself. His wrist and ankles were secured firmly by thick plastic ties to the heavy dining room chair in the extravagantly furnished dining room. It made no sense complaining to her at the opposite end of the long oak table because she was in the same position.

"She has our baby Thadeous; I did what I was told to do!" his wife shot back in a muted whisper through clenched teeth.

Mrs. Frank wasn't one to sass her husband, especially since he provided her lavish lifestyle. She turned a blind eye to all his indiscretions but had no doubt his insatiable greed was the cause of the current predicament.

Thadeous Frank was about as straight as a circle. In the real world people seek trustworthiness and honesty in a C.P.A. but in the underworld corruption is a virtue. Mr. Frank had a knack for taking duffle bags of dirty, filthy, drug blood money and bringing it back crisp and clean. On average, he ran a hundred mil through his financial washing machine annually.

He took a generous ten percent for his trouble. He proved true the adage of no honor among thieves by skimming a few more points off here and there. He didn't have much respect for his black and Latino customers and assumed they wouldn't miss it. Most didn't but Casper did. He may have been the boss of the Black Mob but he was neither black nor stupid. He wrote the first loss off as an oversight but the next time the money was short he sent someone to collect.

"Please Thad, give her what she wants! She has our Jacinthia!" Philomina Frank pleaded.

"Look she'll never find it. Never! Once she gets tired of looking I'll give her a few grand from the safe and let her scurry along," he shot back. Baby or no baby he had no plans of coming off that cash. He liked the kid and all, but she wasn't worth ten million to him.

"Please, it's been hours. Jacinthia must be terrified," Mrs. Frank moaned looking at the kitchen door where the intruder took her child.

"Stop bitching, you're making too much out of it. What can that girl do?" he said curtly. Thadeous was smug like that, confident, always in charge. The silly man had no idea who was upstairs in their home searching for stolen money.

"You're good! I still can't find it!" the intruder sang in the singsong manner of an eight year old as she breezed back into the dining room.

The couple both frowned at the sexy maid outfit she had changed into but for different reasons. The high priced item was cut low in front and high enough in back to show the pert caramel ass in a thong underneath. Thadeous recalled the one time his pasty white wife wore it for him and it didn't look like that.

"Is she wearing my lingerie?" Mrs. Frank complained to her husband then turned to the girl. "Where did you get that?"

"Same place I got this," she giggled and produced a large brown dildo. Brown from the porn star who modeled for it. The white lady turned beet red from embarrassment.

"Well I never!" she huffed indignantly.

The intruder frowned dubiously, sniffed the vibrator, and gave it a flick from her tongue. "Yes you have," the girl giggled sheepishly. She looked at her target and covered her mouth suddenly coy. "Oh I see you!"

"Frank!" Philomina shouted seeing her husband's stubby little erection standing up.

"Here relax," the uninvited guest said turning the knob at the base of the dildo. She giggled again when it began to vibrate with a soft buzz. She shoved it under the woman's vagina and tuned towards the kitchen with Thadeous' eyes glued to her ass.

"How's Jacinthia? She must be hungry," Mrs. Frank asked desperately.

"I doubt it," the girl laughed over her shoulder as she left the room. "We'll talk more after dinner."

"Just give her what she wants! I said nothing about your affairs and…stuff," she demanded trying to ignore the building pleasure the vibrator was creating.

"She said we'll talk after dinner. She hasn't found anything in the…" he paused to look at the grandfather clock, "four hours she's been here! I'll give her ten grand and she can run off and buy some crack and colorful clothes those niggers love so much!"

Mrs. Frank missed the last sentence from the buzzing between her legs. She shook her head 'no' as she tried in vain to stave off an orgasm. It was futile and she came with a loud grunt. It was the best orgasm she'd had with her husband in the same room. Then she concentrated and went for seconds. Her pleasure was cut short before she got to bust another nut.

"Dinner is served," the girl announced pushing the sterling silver dinner cart into the dining room. On it were two plates topped by silver domes to keep the food warm.

"Would you mind loosening our hands so that we may partake in this wonderful meal?" Mr. Frank requested sweetly. He attempted to hide his devious plan behind the kind words and pasted on smile. The fifty-ish out of shape white man figured he could over-power the little girl. Boy was he wrong.

"Um...ok but one at a time," she relented. Thadeous again watched her firm ass shift as she skipped into the next room.

She returned a few seconds later with the black satchel she came with. Before she opened it, she pulled the blonde dreadlock wig off and stretched her neck in relief. It made a dense thud when she placed it on the table. She un-zipped the bag and pulled out a long chrome pistol and even longer chrome silencer. "In case you try anything."

The girl next pulled a pair of wire snips and danced over to the Mrs. She cut the plastic tie that had broken into her skin from her movements. The woman immediately snatched the vibrator from between her legs.

"Ladies first," the server said placing the plate on the table in front of her. She removed the dome with an air of flair complete with, "Ta dah!"

"Oh!" Mrs. Frank uttered at the attractive meal on the good china. She also noticed how pretty the girl was now that her face was no longer obscured by the dreads. She was the exact same shade that the lady took her coffee with milk, not cream. Although her features were delicate and defined, she had an odd look in her eyes. The far-away gaze of a lunatic. The curious gape of the deranged.

"We have wild brown rice with slivers of almond. Braised Brussel sprouts in butter-garlic sauce and I'm sorry but I can't pronounce the meat. Jaza or jasm? Something like that," the girl explained.

Philomina was scared the food would be poisoned but she was more afraid of the big pistol on the table. After a second of contemplation, she decided to eat. She popped a whole Brussel sprout in her mouth and chewed. A slow nod of approval began as she savored the flavor. Next, she sampled the rice and finally the pretty kabobs of meat and peppers.

"How's my baby?" Mrs. Frank asked after swallowing.

"You tell me," the chef asked in return.

"I don't follow?" she frowned curiously.

"You said how's my baby and I said you tell me. That's what you're eating. I didn't over cook her did I?"

"Noooo!" the mother screamed as the nightmare was multiplied times infinity. She pulled and tugged at the plastic tie cutting deeply into her wrist. "You're sick! Sick!"

5

"Me? You're the one who ate her baby lady," the girl shot back sarcastically. With the woman busy trying to cut her own hand off she turned her attention to Mr. Frank. "Have some? It's thigh, I hear that's the best part. I wouldn't know cuz I don't eat kids. Well…"

"Mm mm!" Thadeous declined squeezing his mouth tight and moving his head from side to side to avoid the forkful of baby thigh meat, she extended.

"Ooh, I know what will make you open up," she exclaimed cheerfully at her bright idea. She grabbed the gun a fired a silent round into his calf. Harmless, but it got him to open his mouth wide in an opera worthy high note.

"Good?" she asked shoving the meat inside the open mouth. She didn't wait for an answer and went back into her black bag. Thadeous took the opportunity to spit his kid onto the marble floor.

Both Franks were dealing with their problems but the next item out of the bag took precedence. She stopped thrashing about and he longer felt the burn of the gunshot.

"What the hell is that?" Thadeous demanded as its mere presence offended him. Actually, it should have.

"This," she began, holding up the circular wire contraption, "it's the D.C. 2000! That's short for decapitator 2000. I saw it in a movie and had to have it!"

She went on to explain how the spring-loaded wire hoop snapped shut to a zero circumference when activated. It was strong enough to cut through a 2x4 so skin and bones were no problem at all.

"Now I'm going to cut both of your heads off," she said plainly, as if it were no big deal.

"Why both of our heads? I don't have anything to do with any of this!" Mrs. Frank pleaded in an attempt to save herself.

"No, both of his heads I meant," the girl explained going back into the satchel. The garden shears she produced needed no explanation.

"Wait! Wait! Wait!" Thadeous appealed as she approached. "I'll tell you where the money is!"

"Too late," she said slipping the D.C. 2000 over his head. "I'm glad you didn't give it to me."

"Go to hell!" he shouted and in a final act of defiance, spit in her face. The lovely little lunatic smiled, licked the saliva from around her mouth, and picked up his flaccid penis.

"Ok, bye-bye," she sang and simultaneous hit the switch and closed the shears. The tiny dick head popped off and rolled under his chair. A second later, his big, bald head fell into his lap.

Mrs. Frank stared on in stunned silence as her husband was decapitated. Whoever the girl was, she was a killer. A killa, a real animal. She let out a sigh of contentment and accepted her fate.

"Well, time to go with your baby, but don't tell her you ate her," she whispered conspiratorially.

Mrs. Frank lifted her chin prepaid to die with dignity. Instead of shooting her or cutting any parts off, the girl prepared to leave. She packed her pistol and D.C. 2000 into the bag along with the shears. She took the wire cutters into the kitchen and cut the gas line leading to the restaurant size stove. Then she breezed back through the dining room ignoring the confused woman.

The girl made a stop in the family room and lit the fireplace. Once the gas made it that far the house would be leveled by the explosion. A sly smile spread over her face as she stepped over the body of the butler. He had smiled brightly when he opened the door for her and she shot him in it.

When she got into her SUV and drove away, she added the two kills to her tally. The total was now 99 and she wasn't quite 21. She pulled her cell phone out to report in to the boss.

Casper smiled brightly when he saw the name on his caller ID.

"Yolo! Did you get it?" the white boss of the Black Mob asked eagerly. He didn't need the money but didn't want anyone to have the satisfaction of stealing his and enjoying it.

"No, he wouldn't tell me," she replied sadly. "Good news though. The D.C. 2000 works like a charm!"

"That is good news. Have fun?" Casper inquired.

"I did. I did," Yolo said bouncing in her seat.

A thunderous roar rocked the SUV and shook the earth. A glance in the rearview mirror showed a huge orange fireball where the house once stood.

"Yay! One hundred!" she cheered knowing Mrs. Frank was in the debris blown sky high.

You may wonder why a girl would derive such joy from killing people and the answer is because she's crazy. You may also wonder how she amassed such a high body count at such a young age. The answer to that is simple too; she started early.

Chapter 1

"Here we go again!" the ER doctor groaned as the patient was wheeled in near death. The middle-aged white man didn't care much for black people and he particularly loathed poor people. So this poor black woman was the scum of the earth to him. The fact that she was pregnant only made matters worse.

"Great, another ghetto bastard! World get ready, here comes Leroy Johnson!" he quipped to the amusement of one of the two nurses present.

The white nurse didn't necessarily like the racist jokes but she did like the doctor so she went along with his jokes. The black nurse hated him, his jokes, and his cavalier attitude. And since her peer thought it was funny, fuck her too.

"She's in labor," Nurse Marquita announced hoping to spur some urgency in her co-workers. They stood back while she attempted to wash the emaciated little crack head on the gurney.

The dirt on her skin was clearly visible once her filthy clothes were cut off. Even the smell emanating from the woman could be seen like the ripples of heat emanating from an Arizona highway. Her frail body housed a misshapen lump, the body of her premature baby that was near death, in her belly.

"Her blood pressure is through the roof!" Nurse Nancy said after inflating the arm cuff. She pulled yet another mask over her mouth and nose to avoid the suffocating stench coming from between the patient's legs.

"Why prolong the inevitable? Just let them die," the doctor suggested in violation of both the Hippocratic Oath and humanity.

"If you don't attend to this patient like you would any other patient I will report you!" Marquita growled.

"Oh ok!" he relented before doubling his mask and gloves and moving in. He shoved his whole hand inside the woman's beat up vagina to see how far she had dilated. Her vagina was so loose that it was laid open like a baked potato therefore his hand went in to the wrist with no problem. "Huh?"

"No way!" Nurse Nancy said as the Dr. pulled out a whole condom, a piece of another, and a bottle top. She just shook her head at the mess on the stretcher. The crack addict still had twigs and leaves in her matted hair from sleeping in the woods like a squirrel.

"Yes, it's in labor. The baby's coming," he said as he backed away.

The bells and whistles began going off as the mother's life slipped away. That gave the doctor an excuse to sit back and watch them die. Nurse Marquita couldn't sit idle. She rushed over and shoved her hand inside.

"It's breached, I have the feet!" she screamed just as the mother flat lined.

"One down, one to go," the doctor mumbled dryly. Marquita didn't respond, instead she snatched the child out of its dead mother by its feet. She was then faced with yet another dilemma upon seeing the umbilical cord was wrapped tightly around its neck. The child's face was blue from lack of oxygen. The nurse quickly grabbed a scapula to cut the cord away. Then risking her own life she breathed directly into the child's mouth.

"Marquita that woman is a registered HIV patient! She has full blown AIDS and hasn't picked up her meds in months!" Nurse Nancy warned.

The blue baby took her first breath just as the mother took her last. Nurse Marquita cut and tied the cord to prepare the child for the incubator where she would spend the first few months of her life.

"Well, congratulations, another ward of the state is born. Welcome yet another burden for the tax payers," the doctor bitched.

"Guess you can do the honors and name her. She certainly can't," Nancy said as she pulled a sheet over the corpse.

"Oh, here we go with another 13-syllable ghetto name!" the doctor cackled.

"Oh do you remember the twins?" Nurse Nancy reminded as she cracked up.

"Denise and De-nephew! How could I forget!" he howled. Even Marquita had to stifle a chuckle at the memories of the gold tooth patient who birthed them.

"How about Ephemeral, since it probably won't survive," Nancy offered seriously. The baby was weak, underweight, malnourished, and most likely HIV positive.

"Well you only live once," Marquita said finally noticing the sex of the baby. "Isn't that right Yolo?"

"Yolo Jackson!" the doctor repeated with a decimating nod as if checking the sound of it. "Nice ring to it."

"Yolo Jackson it is," she said and took the child to the neonatal unit to die.

Only she didn't die. To everyone's surprise, the child was spared from the deadly virus that killed her young mother. She gained weight quickly and grew healthier by the day.

However, the stoic infant never smiled, laughed, or cooed. Instead, she wore a perturbed look on her face as if she wanted to curse.

Nurse Marquita wanted to adopt the child but her busy schedule had no room for an infant. Besides, it wouldn't be much of a story if she had since the nurse would have provided the loving home and proper guidance a child needs to be well balanced. Instead she was going into the fucked up foster care system of New York. Blame them; it's their fault that she grew up to be a lunatic.

Chapter 2

Young Yolo was passed from one abusive, dysfunctional foster home to the next. She picked up all kinds of bad habits, curse words, grime, and crime along the way. By four years old, she was on her way to being pretty fucked up, but the next stop went from bad to worse. The Brown residence was about as bad as it gets. It was both bad and worse.

Wyandanch, New York is in the middle of Long Island. The once industrial suburban town was once a premier place for middle class blacks. Once the jobs dried up so did the town. It was quickly reduced to a suburban ghetto. What can be worse than slums in the suburbs?

The town had a booming drug trade and the murder rate that comes with it. As always, the drug trade creates sub-markets. Beer, blunts, and lighters were all good sellers but pussy was a top contender. Intoxicants breed licentious so it was no surprise. Niggas get high and they wanna bust a nut. It's only right.

She-Ra Brown ran the town's brothel. The hard drinking, bare-knuckle fighting lesbian lived with her dim witted, blockhead twin sons Harry and Larry. They were supposed to be security but were more for show since they wouldn't bust a grape in a winery. Besides, their mother was an extremely dangerous person in her own right.

The part-time stud had an inch long clit that made it look like her vagina was giving a 'thumbs up.' She called it her dick and if you have a dick, you're gonna want to get it sucked. No way around it. Her sons had dicks and that's the only thing that made them males. They were too sorry to ever be considered men.

She-Ra saw all the free fucking in town and harnessed it. The local girls and women fucked for beer and blunts so she provided all the beer and blunts they could consume. In exchange, they fucked and sucked on demand. She sold shots of pussy, head, and homemade liquor. She even had her own version of the glory-hole. It was a hole cut in the side of a closet and for ten bucks; you could insert your erection and get a nut. Now who was in the closet was a different story. More often than not, it was some faggot killing two birds with one stone. Sucking dick and making money at the same time. Win/win for a sissy.

Harry and Larry was paid pussy for allowance. Once a week their mother forced one of the prostitutes to fuck them. That didn't keep them from sticking their dicks in the hole every chance they got. She-Ra knew but didn't say anything. Instead, she held it against them internally.

When the opportunity to take in a foster child came up, she jumped at the chance. Not only did the kid come with a check and food stamps, she could use a good bartender. Those sons of hers couldn't fix a drink to save their lives.

They all fell in love with the pretty girl when she arrived. She had a pretty caramel complexion from her late white father. He caught AIDS turning a trick with her mother and took it home to his wife. She died too.

The twins openly gawked at the child when she arrived. It didn't take a mind reader to know what was on their little minds.

"I see you. You better not touch her!" She-Ra told Harry when she caught him glaring at her little backside as she taught her how to mix drinks.

"You let us fuck the other one," Harry pouted. It was true that she turned a blind eye when her sons routinely raped the other foster girls they had.

"That's because they were older!" she snapped. She left out it was conditioning for her to turn them to turning tricks. Most ran away to worse lives, some died in the house. They too were reported as runaways.

"This one is a virgin. I'm sell that little cherry for top dollar the second it gets ripe," she continued as if the child weren't present. No matter, she didn't understand any of it yet anyway.

"We won't fuck her," Larry threw in causing his twin to snicker at the word play. She-Ra was as sharp as the knives in her closet and caught it too.

"Don't fuck and don't touch! I'll bust your fucking head if you do! Don't end up like your sister," she warned.

The reference to their sister sucked the air out of the room. She was technically still in the house albeit buried under a concrete slab in the basement. That was before She-Ra learned a better way to dispose of the bodies. The sassy girl had gotten her throat cut in that same kitchen for back talking.

"Ok," they sang together like they had been doing since they were boys. Just like then they were lying and fondled the girl every chance they got. That was how it started. That was also around the time Yolo witnessed her first murder.

Chapter 3

Walter Thomas was a regular at She-Ra's bar and whorehouse. He routinely came to get drunk and get off. His habit of being belligerent forced She-Ra to whoop his ass and toss him out on several occasions. His disrespect of the girls got him banished from the rooms. He was forced to use the glory hole when he wanted relief. And isn't that what a good nut is, relief?

"Get it! Get it! Bitch get it!" Ol' Walt cheered as he humped the hole in the wall. He slammed his scrawny frame against the wall with every stroke. He still swigged his gin bottle.

Yolo occasionally looked over at him but was much more interested in the violent movie on the TV. Her foster brothers fed her a steady diet of sex and violence. Not just on the screen, the idiots pulled out their penises in front of her on a daily basis. It was nothing for them to masturbate while watching a movie. So she knew what was about to happen, when Walt threw his skinny hips into overdrive.

"Yeah bitch!" Walt yelled and went stiff as he reached a drunken orgasm. It was a good one but he still wasn't satisfied. He pulled his drunken erection out of the hole and looked around. "I'm ready to fuck something! I want some pussy!"

He stared at the twins in his drunken double vision but they didn't have vaginas. He shook his head 'no' at Yolo because she was a child. Walt was some bullshit but he was no pedophile.

"Who in here?" Walt demanded pounding on the closet door. "I'm tryna fuck!"

"Wait for it," Larry laughed as he tried to open the door. There was a brief tug of war between Walt and the occupant of the closet.

"Ah!" Pretty Ricky screamed when he lost the battle of the doorknob. The naked sissy covered his chest as if he actually had breasts. He made good money in that closet anonymously sucking dicks.

"Huh?" Walt asked wondering if it was some kind of magic trick that turned the girl into a guy. He frowned and looked through the hole his dick was just in and still saw the guy. "I ain't no faggot!"

"Yeah you are," Harry laughed cracking his brother up as well. "You just got head from a dude!"

"Who else in there?" he asked snatching the sissy aside. When he found no one else, he turned on his heels and marched down the hall towards She-Ra's room. Harry was about to try and stop him but his brother stopped him.

"Let him go, this gon' be funny!" Larry giggled like a child.

She-Ra had her head between a girl named Tisha's big yellow thighs. She had been trying to bed her for months and finally got the pussy, her tongue twirled like a tornado as she

20

Yolo

worked her magic. The girl whimpered softly as she bust a nut right before the door was kicked in.

"I want some pussy! I ain't no faggot, and I want some pussy!" Walt demanded in a wobbly drunken stance. He set his eyes on She-Ra's ass and made up his mind. "I'm fucking you!"

"Walt," She-Ra began in a slow and deadly cadence. Her chin was dripping from the girl's vagina juice and she was still thrusting her pelvis up at her to make her continue. "Get out."

"I will not! I wanna fuck and you gonna fuck me," he insisted looking at her unused box. The long time lesbian hadn't had sex since she got pregnant with the twins in another life.

The twins, followed by Yolo had all come down the hall to watch the show. They all had gotten in trouble for interrupting She-Ra during one of her carpet munching adventures. Let's face it, it's just plain rude to interrupt someone while eating vagina.

"I won't tell you again," She-Ra warned. The malice in her voice was missed by Walter and Tisha.

"No! I wanna get fucked!" he insisted. Even stomped his feet as an exclamation point.

"Ok you wanna get fucked?" She-Ra growled as she stood from between the thick thighs. All eyes shot to the wet box so no one saw She-Ra pull the tiny .22 from the nightstand. She spun and put a bullet right between Walt's eyes. He did not look happy as death rudely interrupted his life. He wanted to say something but a bullet to the brain has a way of stealing one's train of thought. "Now you're fucked!"

As soon as he dropped dead She-Ra turned and shot the girl. The vagina tasted wonderful but could she keep quiet about the murder? Guess she will now huh?

"Harry put Walt in the tub. Yolo, grab my brown satchel out of the closet," she ordered.

As soon as Larry was left alone with the dead, he began to play in the still wet box. If he had the time, he would have climbed inside of her. The nasty bastard.

"What we gonna do with him? Yolo asked curiously at the corpse. With that question went the last of her innocence. Walt stared up with dead eyes as if he were wondering the same thing.

"We..." She-Ra said taking the heavy bag from her and opening it. "Are going to cut him up. Time you learn how to dispose of a body properly."

She-Ra selected a large knife with a wooden handle. Its super sharp blade glistened in the florescent light as she held it up for inspection. It got her approval in the form of a head nod.

"We always start with the penis," she began and took a grip of the still semi-erect dick at the base, under the balls. She didn't explain why to start with the dick so I won't speculate. I'm just an author after all, what would I know about cutting up bodies?

The trio came off easily with one pass of the blade. They had been hanging together their whole lives so it was only right that they were tossed in the bucket together.

"I'll let you do the next penis," She-Ra offered in consolation.

"Ok!" Yolo cheered and clapped at the prospect. "Yay!"

"It's just like chicken," she explained as she put the blade under Walters's armpit and sawed off his wing. It was indeed just like she taught the girl to cut up chicken. She still had plenty more to teach the child. She planned to groom her to please both men and women. She-Ra started the cut under the next arm and let Yolo take over.

"Like that?" Yolo asked eagerly when the limb fell off. "It is just like chicken!"

She-Ra took back over and took Walter apart. His head was last and he still didn't look happy. She thought it would be cute to stuff his dick into the mouth and put it back in the bag. Yolo sure got a kick out of it and snickered.

"Harry! Larry!" She-Ra yelled interrupting her sons from molesting the dead girl. Harry was playing in her vagina with one hand and himself with the other while Larry got some dead head. "Come get this one and bring the next one."

Yolo took the lead in taking Tisha apart. She didn't look happy either when her head went into the bag. That was the first time she witnessed murder but it would not be the last.

Chapter 4

Age seven is generally the age of discernment for most children. A new age of enlightenment, a new age of toys and games. Yolo was no exception, except her new game was murder. As any killer will tell you, that first one is the most memorable. Most killers actually forget a victim here or there but they always remember that first one. Everyone remembers losing their cherry.

Speaking of cherries, She-Ra was still protecting Yolo's with threats of extreme violence. The girl grew prettier by the day and the idiot twins lusted after her peeking in on her at bath time or while she slept. They pulled their dicks out on her so much she was growing a hatred for that particular appendage.

Yolo also had a new friend in the new girl who just moved on the block. Jane was the same age, in her same class, and attached herself.

She was fussy little girly girl who loved to dictate everything they did. Yolo tolerated her so she could have company her own age. The local prostitutes liked to play in her sandy hair and teach her sexual stuff that amused but didn't interest her.

Harry had been put on prostitute probation for one infraction or another. He stood behind Yolo and Jane looking up their little dresses while masturbating. High off liquor and loud he could no longer contain himself. When Yolo went to use the bathroom, he rushed in behind her.

Yolo tried to scream when he attacked but that only opened the way for what he was trying to do. She fought the oral rape valiantly but the grown man was just too strong for her. She was disgusted from the start but it got worse at the end. It felt like he was peeing in her mouth but she knew enough to know better.

"And you better not tell She-Ra either. You do and I'll kill yo' little ass," he warned knowing death was the fate that awaited him if she did tell.

"I'm not telling nobody nothing. I'm going to kill you and cut you up," she vowed. Yolo was too angry for tears. She didn't want comfort; she wanted revenge. A red rage consumed her soul like a wild fire. The whispers of Satan and evil Jinn reverberated in her young mind. They called for blood and blood they would get.

"Oh what you got going on?" Larry asked jealously when he saw his brother coming out of the bathroom. He saw him putting his dick away while Yolo stood behind him.

"Little bitch got some good head!" Harry bragged. His twin was as sick as he was and got excited.

"My turn!" he cheered as if this was the 'pedophile-go-round' at a child molester convention. He shoved his brother aside and rushed in to rape her too.

"Harry! Larry! Y'all bring your sorry asses out here. I told you we're going shopping," She-Ra yelled thus prolonging at least one of her sons' lives. One was dying that day.

"Shit!" Larry spat, stomping his foot. "I'll see you when we get back."

"What took you so long? What's wrong with you? Why is your hair messed up? Why is your lip bleeding? You look funny. Why you..." Jane rambled when Yolo returned. It was her normal everyday babble but that wasn't the day.

"Argh!" Yolo grunted as she struck. She snatched the sash from Jane's dress and wrapped it around her neck. The silly child was still trying to ask questions as she was choked to death.

"What's wrong with you? Why your hair messed up? Blah, blah, blah," Yolo teased the corpse. She calmly sat down and resumed playing with the dolls now that the girl had finally shut up.

Yolo was in a slight panic when she heard the car pull up hours later. She had been having so much fun without Jane's silly rules and banter that she forgot about her. She-Ra scolded her enough about leaving toys laying around. So she knew she would freak out about dead friends laying out. Yolo jumped up and drug the body out of sight.

"Jane gone?" She-Ra asked when she found Yolo playing alone in the den.

"She's gone alright," she replied stifling a giggle. Already she found murder amusing. Her smile dissipated quickly when she saw Larry glaring at her lustfully.

"Come on and help with dinner," She-Ra ordered and Yolo quickly complied. The twins went to smoke themselves silly while dinner was being prepared.

She-Ra was delighted to have another girl to train and teach. She taught her all the tricks and trades of being a criminal as well as cooking and cleaning. Things she taught her own daughter before she killed her. Those skills were buried along with her in the basement. Every time Yolo cut up a chicken, she remembered old Walt.

"This looks like a baby," Yolo giggled at the sight of a plump hen laying naked on the counter. She slipped the sharp knife between the limbs and easily removed them.

She washed, seasoned, and then dropped the pieces in the pan of sizzling oil. A stern knock on the door put a frown on her face as she glanced up at the wall clock. It was too early for the whores and customers to arrive. She listened as one of her dumb sons lumbered towards the door.

"It's the police!" Larry shouted in a whisper with his eyes wide as dinner plates. He knew the beat cops often stopped through for shots of liquor or a dip in the glory hole but it was too early still.

"Calm down Scarface," She-Ra laughed wiping the flour on her apron. It wasn't like they had anything to worry about since they were too dumb to hustle. "I may need you to jump in the closet for a few minutes though," She-Ra laughed as she went to the front door.

"Jump in the closet!" Harry laughed and pointed at his brother. It would be his last good laugh for some time to come.

"How can I help you boys?" She-Ra asked like the sweet little lady she wasn't. Her pasted on phony smiled evaporated in an instant when she saw all the police activity on the block. It was flooded with cops; k-9 and a news van had just pulled to a stop. "What's going on?"

"Missing kid. Jane Patterson didn't come home," the first cop said looking past her into the house. Only he was looking for girls, not the girl. Being a regular, he hoped to get off real quick while everyone else searched.

"That's my daughter friend. She was here earlier. Yolo!" She-Ra turned and yelled. "What time did your friend go home?"

Yolo just shrugged her shoulders in reply causing the second cop to step and speak up. "We better come have a look."

"Missing children are a big deal and the media is here. We gotta check every house on the block," the first cop explained apologetically.

"As long as you're just looking for the girl," She-Ra chuckled nervously. She didn't know the new guy and didn't want him stumbling upon her illegal activities.

"Just a quick peek," he replied with a reassuring wink. His partner saw it and was put on alert.

"Well come on in," She-Ra smiled and stepped aside so they could enter. To her relief the regular cop offered to take the front of the house and sent his partner to the rear.

The front room contained black jack tables, a roulette wheel, and cash bar. All illegal to operate on Long Island. The bedrooms were basically clean since they were mainly used to turn tricks. There was a nice supply of assorted pills in She-

Ra's room along with a couple of guns. She might have to put one of her sons in the closet after all.

Larry's room was the first down the hall so it was the first one searched. A look under the bed and in the closet showed he had a taste for porn but no child. The next two rooms were used to turn tricks but no child. When he got to Harry's room he repeated the process but got different results. When he reached the closet, he got the shock of his life.

"What the...?" he asked. Jane stared up at him with lifeless eyes. She of course couldn't answer so he scrambled to pull both his gun and his radio. He was so shook up by his discovery that he yelled into his service weapon instead of the radio.

"10-99! I...oops," he said before switching to the radio and trying again. "10-99, I found her! I found her!" He rushed out and laid the family down at gunpoint.

"What's going on?" his partner asked in a panic.

"The girl's in the closet dead!"

A second later, the house was over-run with police and emergency workers. The Brown family was all cuffed sitting in the living room. All but Yolo of course since she was a kid. Once it was determined, that it was Harry's room; he was carted off to the precinct.

The angry mob murmured death threats when he emerged and was led to a police car. A hundred years ago, he would have been killed on the spot. New York has the death penalty so they would have to wait a little longer. In a sense, he was

Yolo's second victim of the day but not the last. The night was still young after all.

A collective groan was heard when the small body bag was brought out. Mrs. Patterson swooned and fainted at the sight. It was a heart wrenching sight that reached down to the soul. Not Yolo's soul though, she could give a fuck. The girl talked too much but hadn't said a word since she died. With supervisors on hand, the pills and pistol in She-Ra's room couldn't be ignored. It was enough to ger her arrested, but she wouldn't go to prison for it.

"Call the lawyer so he can get me a bail," She-Ra instructed her son as she too was led away.

"Ok Mommy, right away!" he shot back like he was going to do it. He wasn't. The second the house was cleaned of police, he turned to Yolo.

"Finally got you alone," Larry growled grabbing his erection through his pants. "I need my dick sucked."

"Suck it yourself!" Yolo shot back. She glanced around the room for weapons but didn't see any. Knowing he wasn't smarter than a fifth grader, she would out smart him. It wouldn't be hard. A few of the houseplants could probably out smart him.

"I can't! I would if I could," he admitted. He sure tried to suck his own dick on a couple of occasions but came up short both literally and figuratively. "You did Harry now you gotta do me!"

Salam

"Ok but you gotta let me tie you up first like he did," Yolo replied. She seen enough sexuality to know licking her lips was a good look so she did. It did the trick too.

"Ok!" Larry cheered. He was so thirsty he forgot seeing them come out of the bathroom and he wasn't tied up. "Come on!"

Dumb ass led her to his room and stripped naked. He climbed in the middle of the bed with his erection sticking straight up in the air. He showed Yolo how to tie a knot and secured his own wrist to the headboard.

"Like this?" Yolo asked as she attempted to repeat the process on the other wrist. When she gave it a tug, it came a loose in her hand.

"No you gotta go over, then under. Ok now pull it tight," he coached. She followed his directions and gave it a firm tug.

"Yay!" she cheered happily when it didn't come loose. "Now the ankles! I'll be right back" Yolo sang and skipped from the room.

"Where you going? I need my dick sucked," Larry insisted humping the air. He was still thrusting his hips upwards when Yolo returned dragging the satchel. He knew exactly what was in it and stopped mid-hump. Even his erection knew what was in the bag and deflated instantly.

"W...w...w...w...w... wait!" Larry begged then switched gears to bully. "Un-tie me right now! Right now I say!"

"W...w...w...wa...un-tie me right now," Yolo mocked as she dug in the bag. Larry really tried to pull free when that big shiny blade came into view. "You gotta start with the penis you know?"

"No, no you don't! You don't!" he pleaded. Wasted his breath is more like it because Yolo grabbed the flaccid dick and got to work.

She soon found out that cutting the dick off a live man is very different from a dead guy. First, there is the howl. Larry let out a scream that was a cross of a zebra giving birth, an injured opera singer, and a man getting his dick cut off while still alive.

Then there is the blood. A blast of hot blood splashed her face and open mouth once she managed to hack it off. Her technique wasn't yet what it will be by the end of this story. She actually accidentally left one of his balls on. I guess it's a ball technically since it's all by itself. Instead of being repulsed by the sight, smell, and feel of the blood, she played in it.

"Oh!" Yolo said remembering Larry wanted some head. She moved up and worked his own dick in and out of his mouth, "Like that?"

Larry of course didn't answer. For one he had his dick in his mouth and two; he was dying. Once his clock stopped, she got to work cutting him up. Just like a chicken, she started with the wings. Then the leg quarters and finally the head. Larry's big ass head rolled off the bed and landed with a thud. She hoped to be able to dispose of the body before She-Ra got home but no such luck.

"Larry! Get yo sorry ass out here!" She-Ra yelled as she stormed back into the house.

Chapter 5

"Larry! Larry! Get your sorry ass out here! Why didn't you call the lawyer?" She-Ra yelled. When no reply came, she went in his room screaming his name. She eventually found him but he wasn't how she left him.

"What did you do?" she asked Yolo when she walked into Larry's room. The child was covered head to toe in dried black blood and the air was thick with the distinct coppery smell of blood. "Where is my son?"

"Um…" Yolo stammered, looking for an explanation. But what's to explain? The man was in six pieces, seven counting the dick in his mouth. She just huffed and pulled the comforter away.

"You little lunatic!" were the last words Yolo heard before the attack. She-Ra beat the girl as if she were a grown man. She punched, kicked, clawed, and body slammed her like it was Monday night wrestling. Except this was real, a real beat down.

She-Ra was actually shocked the little girl lived through the beating. It was on the way to the tub to cut her up that she discovered she still had a pulse. She had no idea that the child was born dead and it would take a lot more than that to kill her. She-Ra dumped her in the bed and set out on the gruesome task of cutting up her son properly.

When Yolo fully recovered, she got beat into a coma. When she recovered from that beating, she got another and another as she entered a new age of abuse. Not only did she get her ass kicked on a regular bases but was forced to pick up on the twins duties around the house. She cut grass and chopped wood growing stronger and angrier by the day. All the while, she was warned that her body would be sold as soon as she turned ripe. She had no idea what that meant until the day came.

"She-Ra! She-Ra!" a frantic Yolo called as she pounded on her foster mother's door. She knew the woman had company and what she was doing with her company but this was an emergency. She was bleeding! When no reply came, she turned the knob and barged in.

"Girl...don't...you...see I'm...busy!" She-Ra replied not wanting to stop working over her new friend Britney's box.

"But I'm bleeding! My stuff is bleeding," she whined confused by what was going on. The little nubs on her chest had begun to itch lately as well.

"What stuff? Where?" She-Ra asked as she reluctantly rose from the bushy vagina. She looked down and saw blood on Yolo's little cotton panties. "Ooh that's what we've waiting on!"

"Little mama you a woman now," She-Ra's guest cheered.

"Yup, that cherry just got ripe. Go on and run a bath, I'll be in once I finish in here," She-Ra said and muff dived back in.

Yolo

Yolo followed directions and got in the tub. She
washed with a sense of dread as she figured out what was to
come. Now that she had begun to develop, She-Ra was going
to sell her. Sell her virginity as if it was hers to sell. It wasn't
and Yolo was mad. She moved her toes individually then
fingers and limbs. This was proof that she and not She-Ra
controlled her body. It was her virginity and she decided to
keep it. Even if she hat to kill to do so.

****

"Let me see," She-Ra demanded on a daily basis to
check Yolo's pad. She had to bring a used one to get a fresh
one so she could keep up on her flow. She had a wealthy client
waiting in the wing. A sick little pedophile with ten grand to
spare. It wasn't his money to spare and his ass was about to be
in trouble.

Maurice Wheeler made his money in stocks and bonds.
He flipped it until it multiplied many times over. It afforded
him the lavish home where he kept his trophy wife along with
his other toys and accessories. During a trip to the Dominican
Republic, he stumbled across the disgusting world of
pedophilia. The small Caribbean Island had a bustling child
sex market so he made monthly trips.

Being the enterprising entrepreneur that he was he saw
a hustle in it. It began by selling his homemade footage to
likeminded sick fucks who liked that sick shit. As the market
grew, he decided to dive full steam ahead into child
pornography. Since he couldn't use his legal money to finance
the illicit business, he took out a loan.

He heard about the Black Mob through the
underground grapevine and got the finances. Had Casper

37

known what it was for he would have sent a killer to kill him. Instead, he bought the lie about opening a day care center and cut a check.

It's never wise to borrow money from a loan shark. To make the decision not to pay them back is just plain stupid. Wheeler had stiffed plenty of banks in the past. What's the worst they could do, sue him? The Black Mob didn't sue; they sent collectors. If you didn't come up with what you owe it would cost a whole lot more than you could afford. The target was stalked for weeks until he came out in the open. When he left his home one night, he had an unseen trail.

"Looks like our friend has a hot date!" Casper observed to the very serious man behind the wheel. "Let's see if we can make it a little hotter shall we?"

"We shall," Mr. Grimsly agreed and pulled out behind him.

****

"Now it's gonna hurt a little and it'll be a little blood," She-Ra explained as she prepared Yolo for her Saturday night rape date.

"There's gonna be a lot of blood and it's gonna hurt a lot," Yolo assured her nodding her head in agreement with herself. There was a murderous glint in her eyes but She-Ra was too busy fussing with her pigtails to catch it.

Child molesters like pigtails and bobbie socks so that's exactly how She-Ra dressed her. She had on an Easter Sunday looking dress along with shiny patent leather shoes. Even had a little patent leather purse to match.

Yolo

"He's here!" She-Ra announced and clapped happily when the doorbell chimed. She had them ten thousand dollars spent several times in her mind.

"What is this place?" Mr. Grimsly asked curiously. The doll, flowers, and happy gait of Wheeler made him wonder. Rumors of his sick fetish had just reached them and his blood began to boil.

Mr. Grimsly was a very, very dangerous man. He had been doing hits for a living for most of his life. The aging killer now in his early sixties killed exclusively for the Black Mob. He was deadly efficient but oddly humane. It was the latter trait that his employer could do without. Casper lost his humanity along with his anal virginity. The only obstacle between him and total anarchy was the refined Mr. Grimly. Casper was the boss but still held a fatherly respect for the elderly gentleman.

"Guess we're about to find out," Casper announced and got out of the car. He waited for his companion to collect the tools of his trade than followed Wheeler to the house.

"Mr. Wheeler!" She-Ra gushed pleasantly as she pulled the door open for the child molester. Yolo had a bitter scowl on her face and took the opportunity to move the small revolver she lifted from She-Ra's dildo drawer and conceal it behind her back.

"Miss She-Ra, always a pleas…oh my! Is that her?" he asked fawningly at the sight of the little girl. He knew her to be 10 but she looked seven and that was fine by him. The younger the better was his mantra. Doctors are still examining brains of pedophiles looking for a cure. Seeing her scrawny

39

legs and tiny breast buds had his heart beating a hundred miles a minute.

"Say hello to Mr. Wheeler Yolo," She-Ra urged, through clenched teeth.

"Good-bye Mr. Wheeler," Yolo said with a smirk. Her mind commanded her hands to produce the gun and shoot him but the front door opened first.

"Hello Mr. Wheeler," a male voice said causing all in attendance to turn towards the door. There stood a smiling Casper along with Mr. Grimsly who rarely smiled.

Actually, Grimsly did smile in a past life. Back when he only did part time hits to augment his tool manufacturing shop. He was a happy husband until a burglar killed his wife. Now he only manufactured deadly devices and killed people. He answered an ad in as underground forum and got hooked up with the Black Mob. He was now the in-house killer. Murderer of record so to speak. The bag he carried was just like the one in She-Ra's closet. It contained everything one would need to take a body apart in small pieces. He planned to distribute those pieces to a few other customers with past due balances. It was the Black Mob's version of a collection letter.

"Casper! Hey um… good to see you! I've been trying to call you! Things have been so slow! I'm uh… expecting some receivables next week and will have you all squared away!" Wheeler managed to get out. It actually sounded pretty good, but it didn't match up to the previous lies.

"Is that what he told us last week? It isn't is it?" Casper asked Grimsly with a curious frown.

Yolo

"Not at all," Grimsly replied grimly.

"Yeah, no, it's just that things have been slow and I'm tapped for cash and…"

"So, what's in the bag?" Casper inquired about the cash pouch he clutched in his hand.

"Huh?" Wheeler asked getting a round of laughter and the pouch snatched.

"Huh it's… like ten large here!" he said flipping through the cash with his thumbs. He looked at Wheeler, She-Ra, and then Yolo and figured it out. "Youse a real piece of shit you know! You tryna screw the kid?"

"Screwed you too boss," Grimsly instigated. He wasn't much of a talker and wanted to get to the killing part.

"Did he touch you little girl?" he asked Yolo then turned to She-Ra. "Was you gonna let him touch her?"

"No!" She-Ra shouted feigning outrage. She spoke as if it were the most preposterous thing she'd ever heard. "I would never let anyone touch my child."

"Liar. You was gon' sell my cherry to that man," Yolo growled.

Grimsly heard murder in her tone as she spoke. He spoke that language fluently and easily picked up on it. Sure enough, her little arm came from behind her back. In her little hand was a little pistol.

41

"What are you going to do with that dear?" Grimsly asked softly.

"Kill her for selling me and him for buying me," Yolo stated. So matter of factly no one present doubted her, except Casper that is. He twisted his lips dubiously as if she wouldn't bust a grape.

"Well go on and shoot he- ...damn!" Casper shouted as Yolo shot She-Ra before he could finish the statement. The bullet rushed into her open mouth and entered her brain. She shook her head and dropped dead on the spot.

"Him too?" Yolo said asking for permission.

"No him too!" Wheeler shrieked. He could not believe he just witnessed a child kill someone. Casper looked at a delighted Grimsly who gave a nod. It was his kill but why not.

"Sure you can kill him," Casper said sweetly and watched her put a bullet in the man's forehead.

Wheeler hit the ground twitching so Yolo stood over him and fired into his bald spot twice, then handed over the gun.

"Bring him to the bathroom. I'll get the stuff," Yolo said and walked off towards the rear.

"Well you heard the lady. Take him to the bathroom," Casper laughed. He had no idea what was coming but he was very eager to see.

"Right away boss," Grimsly said just as eagerly. The slight man was still super strong and easily toted Wheeler to the bathroom. He plopped him in the tub just as Yolo arrived with the satchel.

"No way," Grimly exclaimed seeing the tools of the trade. Yolo started with a pair of emergency room scissors and shred his clothes away.

"You gotta start with the penis," Yolo explained and did just that.

"Knew you were a cocksucker!" Casper laughed when the girl stuffed his stuff in his mouth.

"Boss, can I keep her?" Grimsly said with the enthusiasm of a boy finding a turtle in the backyard.

"A pet murderer? You would be the first on the block with one," Casper shrugged. "Guess we gotta, seeing as she killed her mom."

She was able to lop the penis off with one stroke because she had a little practice. Larry may have been her first but Mr. Wheeler was her fourth so she was quite proficient at it. The second was a smart mouth deliveryman who kept disrespecting She-Ra. The foul tempered woman shot him in his temple the second after he installed the flat screen. The third was a local stick up kid who figured the brothel would be an easy lick. Ironically, he was carried out in the same duffle bag he brought to tote his haul.

"Now what?" Grimly asked once the bodies were broken down.

"Um…I don't know?" Yolo admitted. This was as far as she ever got. She had no idea what She-Ra did with the parts.

"I'll show you some other time. I have so much to teach you," Grimly said delighted to have a student. What he did teach her for now was how to use a house against itself. He ruptured a gas line and lit a candle in the room furthest from it. That would give them plenty of time to get away as the home filled with gas. Once the two met, it was...

"Cool!" Yolo cheered at the orange explosion behind them as they drove away. "Can we do it again?"

"Don't worry little lady, we'll be doing that plenty. Trust me."

Chapter 6

"Wow!" Yolo cheered sounding her age when they arrived at the Black Mob mansion. The gated estate was spectacular and the circular driveway was home to a cool million in cool cars.

"Wow," again when they entered the grand foyer of the grand home. Her eyes darted from the marble floors, winding staircase, and extravagant chandelier.

"Come, I'll show you to your room," Grimsly announced and led the way. The large home had several extra rooms so he literally just picked one.

Yolo

"Wow!" Yolo cheered once more at her new digs. It had a generic bedroom set along with TV, computer, and stereo.

"I'll take you shopping for clothes and incidentals in the morning," he said turning to leave. He only took one step before she rushed over.

"Thank you!" she said wrapping her arms around Grimsly. "Thank you for saving me from that place and thank you for letting me kill those people."

"My pleasure," he replied patting her head like a puppy. "Get some sleep."

"Well what are you going to do with her?" Casper asked when Mr. Grimsly found him in the kitchen.

"I'm going to train her. She'll replace me one day. The girl is a natural born killer."

"You should know. If anyone would know it would be you," he said and walked off. Mr. Grimsly was a tea drinker but Casper had a penchant for Vodka so he headed to the den for a shot.

"If it isn't the Baron! No don't get up," Casper teased the green mile look-a-like. The large black man was the official face of the Black Mob even though he didn't have a clue to what they did.

The mute saved Casper's life in prison so Casper vowed to take care of him for the rest of his life. Technically Baron only saved his ass, not his life. The black inmates didn't want to kill him; they wanted to fuck him. Baron couldn't stop him from losing his virginity, but he prevented things from going from bad to worse.

45

Casper really did appreciate it but was rude and nasty because he was a piece of shit. When they got out of prison he used his old connects and the Baron's muscle to flip his money. And flip he did until the Black Mob was a force in every city, hood, ghetto, alley, and side street.

They controlled their legion of dealers, pimps, and killers with extreme acts of violence. This wasn't the run of the mill get down or lay down. No, their mantra was fuck up and get cut up. Into bite size pieces that is. Be a greedy pig and get fed to greedy pigs. Grimsly took great pride in killing. He could kill everyone and everything except the cancer that was slowly killing him.

****

"Rise and shine!" Grimsly ordered pulling the curtains back in Yolo's room. It was merely for show as the sun had yet to rise.

"Ok Mr. Grimsly," Yolo said politely and got out of the bed completely naked.

"Where are your clothes child?" he snapped snapping his head away in embarrassment. She-Ra often had the girl running around naked or nearly naked to where she thought nothing of it. Mr. Grimsly did though; the man was a prude and intended to make a lady out of the girl.

"They burned up with She-Ra," she giggled at both the woman's demise and his blushing.

"Put something on. We're going shopping," he ordered and stepped from the room.

Yolo

Yolo watched the world pass by the car window with the curiosity of someone who didn't get out much. That was because she didn't get out much. Life with She-Ra was fixing drinks and watching various sex acts. She only now realized she was a slave not that she was free.

"How about this?" Yolo asked holding another short skirt to her skinny frame. She wanted to dress like the teen girls she saw in the mall but the stuffy Mr. Grimsly wouldn't hear it.

"If you dress like a lady people will treat you like a lady," he explained correctly. After all, if a woman dresses like a slut how can she expect men to view her any differently? They won't. They'll just call it like they see it. Leaving off the guesswork.

With the help of a sales clerk, they settled on some age appropriate clothing. Yolo got dresses, skirts, jeans, and shirts but more importantly sweats to train in. Once they returned to the mansion, the training began.

Since there was no legal guardian to enroll the child in school she was home schooled. Probably came out better without all the distraction of a bunch of rowdy kids. For six hours a day, the extremely intelligent Mr. Grimsly shared his knowledge of all things secular. After that came Yolo's favorite subject, murder.

"Wow!" Yolo exclaimed when Grimsly finally took her to his underground lair.

His workshop was filled with various devices and contraptions to kill. Guns, knives, garrotes, and even roadside bombs. A fancy tube caught her attention and she rushed over to grab it.

"Oops!" Yolo said when she put her mouth to it and caused a dart to fly out and lodge in the wall.

"Be careful girl!" Grimsly chided and took the blowgun from her hand. "Had you hit me with it you would have been alone in the room in ten seconds!"

To prove his point he pulled the dart from the wall and went to a cage holding several white rabbits. He poked one with the dart and it keeled over dead two seconds later. He picked it up by its obviously unlucky foot and headed over to another cage where a ball python lay curled up. The serpent hissed loudly when the rabbit was dropped in and struck. He quickly wrapped it in its clutches and squeezed. Yolo missed most of what was said after by watching the snake swallow its meal.

As the years ticked by Yolo proved to be an excellent student, she grasped most concepts immediately and locked them in. She even posed poignant question that sometimes stumped her teacher. By 12, she got to get some on the job training but no killing just yet.

"Go!" Grimsly shouted and hit the stopwatch sending Yolo into action.

The girl immediately began to dismember an ex-mob member named Chaves used to run the black tar heroin market in Houston until he got beside himself. I guess it was karma when Yolo sat his head beside himself. Next arms, legs, and …

"Time!" Yolo shouted holding her bloody hands up to show she was finished.

"Not bad," Grimsly said twisting his lips dubiously. It wasn't bad because it was damn good. The girl just tied his personal best. "Bag him, let's go feed the hogs."

"Yay!" Yolo sang clapping her bloody hands joyfully. This would be her first time actually going to the cabin. As soon as Grimsly left her alone, she cut off his dick and shoved it in his mouth for old time's sake. Her teacher made her stop since it served no purpose. She just did it for fun.

Once ol' Chaves was bagged, he was loaded in the truck for the ride out to Pennsylvania. The Black Mob kept a cabin tucked away in the Pocono Mountains. That's where the human garbage disposals lived. The ravenous pigs would eat anything or anyone fed to them. This was how bodies disappeared without a trace.

After school and training ended for the day, Yolo would retreat to her computer for private study. Her two favorite subjects were porn and murder. The effects of living with She-Ra gave her a fascination for sex. She didn't want any but did like to watch. Most times, she found it amusing.

What she liked to read about most were serial killers, mass murderers. Not the cowards who shoot up schools or malls but the real killers. Ramirez, Bundy, Dahmer, and the like. By far her favorite was a mythical murderer from the Bronx called Killa. The man who allegedly blew up a whole funeral home.

She wondered if he wasn't just an urban legend because no pictures of him could be found. Just reports, rumors, and alleged sightings. According to folk lore, the handsome killer killed 100 people by the time he was 21. That became her goal. A search of the 100 kills only produced an ancient but true story…

There was once a bad man who killed 99 men. He decided to repent and seek forgiveness so he sought out a monk. The monk told him there was no forgiving him so he killed him too making it 100 kills in all. He came across a wise man and told him of his plight. The wise man told him to leave his own village of wicked people and migrate to a land filled with righteous people. He set out on that path but died before he reached it.

God sent the Angel of mercy and the Angel of punishment to see who would claim the soul. They settled the debate by measuring the distance between the bad place he left and the place of forgiveness that he sought. God moved him closer to the good land and the angel of mercy claimed him.

"Shoot he killed a hundred men too!" Yolo protested. She obviously missed the point, did you?

Chapter 7

By 16 Yolo was a beautiful young lady. Her petite yet curvy little body disguised her brute strength. A disarmingly pretty smile hid the malice of her little black heart and mid-back long sandy brown hair covered her twisted mind. She was indeed a lovely little lunatic.

Mr. Grimsly had trained her to be quite the murderer. She was proficient in every killing technique known to man not to mention quite a few they invented. By far her favorite was hand-to-hand combat. She perfected the deadly move nicknamed, 'The bitch in you.' It was so painful that it would bring out the bitch in the biggest, baddest bully.

He taught her to be amorphous, a chameleon able to blend into any environment. She could dress up to a twenty something or down to pubescent. She had a variety of wigs including a bulletproof blonde dreadlock number. The cap and thick dreads were made of Kevlar. Grimsly designed several pairs of stiletto heels with daggers concealed in the heel. Oh, and of course there is the D.C. 2000.

She was ready, willing, able, and trained to go. The only thing standing in the way of her kills was...

"No! You are not ready," Grimly answered yet another plea to take the lead on a hit. He had begun taking her along on missions and she was dying to make someone die.

"I'm ready! I'm ready!" she shouted, bouncing in her seat.

"So how would you handle this situation?" he said to test her as they pulled behind their mark at his favorite diner. Today's victim was yet another degenerate gambler. He had more excuses than cash and that wouldn't do. The thing about ass betting is that you eventually have to pay with your ass. He ran out of time, it was time to die.

"I walk in and shoot him in the back of his head and walk out," Yolo said matter of factly. She was ready to hop out and do just that if she got the green light.

"You'll have to shoot the waitress, the cook, and …four or five customers too. No witnesses right?"

"No problem," she shrugged not having a problem with the extra bodies. She did have a quota to meet after all. With only four murders under her belt, she needed 96 more in the next five years. That was an average of 19 a year and she had no problem with it.

"It is a problem, it's extra and unnecessary. NO, we never leave witnesses but we try not to have witnesses," Grimsly lectured. It was all about efficiency for him. No wasted energy or effort. In all the hits, he'd done in his life; there wasn't a single witness. Even when done in public like this one would be.

"Watch the master," the teacher teased as the mark stood and headed to the restroom. Grimsly donned a hat and glasses and walked swiftly into the diner.

Yolo watched intently as Grimsly entered the diner. She just knew he would follow him into the bathroom and leave him slumped in one of the stalls. Instead, he stepped to the counter next to his food and ordered coffee. Yolo couldn't see it but the second the waitress turned her back to fill the cup he pulled a syringe from his pocket. He deftly squirted liquid into his coffee and tucked it away.

"Thank you, come again," the waitress said stoically in a rough smoker's voice. She even showed him her tobacco-stained smile to prove how bad cigarettes are.

Grimsly nodded his head in reply while waving off the change as a tip. He turned to leave just as the mark returned from the restroom. The man sat down and resumed his meal like he did every day. Only today was his last day.

"Why didn't you kill him?" Yolo pouted, sticking her lip out and crossing her arms like a disappointed child. Which in a lot of ways she was.

"I did. Wait for it, wait…for…it," Grimsly said jovially as he sipped and chewed. Just then, he keeled over face first into his sunny side up eggs. "Sodium cyanide. The coroner may or may not find it. Either way he's dead."

****

The next unlucky contestant on the price is wrong was an Amityville drug dealer named Treble. His real name was Trevor but they called him Treble because he had absolutely no bass in his voice. That alone was annoying enough to die for but he was in trouble for violating The Black Mob's F.Y.P.M. rule.

That's an acronym for fuck you, pay me. Problems arise in drug dealing like raids and robberies but that's your problem.

If you got mob dope on credit it doesn't matter what happens, fuck you pay me.

Treble and his crew did have two trap houses raided and a stash spot robbed but fuck you, pay me. Shit happens but instead of working it off or making it up Treble decided to switch connects. A crew of Columbians in Queens filled the void. That too was a no-no that they would have to pay for as well.

"A-yo fuck that little white boy Casper and that big black Baron!" Treble shrieked sounding like Mariah Carey. His crew of childhood friends Reggie, Ace, and Ray all nodded in agreement. They had all grown up together so it was only fitting that they all die together.

Treble was a true hustler and had his town on smash. Amityville, New York is best known for that haunted house but it also has the highest population of crack heads, per capita in the world. The man would be a millionaire if he lived long enough. Only, that wasn't going to happen.

"Yeah fuck 'em!" Ace cosigned like hype-men do. At 6'4" 325, he was kept around for his brawn not brains.

"Fuck 'em," Ray agreed. He was an exceptionally violent man ready for war at all times.

"Yo we fuckin' with the Mob! Let's just pay them and keep it moving," Reggie said cautiously. He heard the rumors of murder and mayhem and wanted no part of it.

"We done voted. The results of the election are three to one in favor of fuck 'em," Treble laughed.

Reggie just shook his head at the unwise decision. He should have done more than just shake his head. He should have moved to Alaska or the moon. His mother used to warn him growing up that hanging with Treble was going to get him in trouble one day. That day was near.

****

"Yolo! If you're coming then come along!" Mr. Grimsly shouted from the den. The cuter the girl got the longer it took for her to get ready. It seems like the opposite would be true. You're cute, so come on.

"Ready," Yolo sang as she breezed into the room giving the stuffy Grimsly a fit with her outfit.

"What do you have on? Where are your clothes!" he demanded turning his head in embarrassment.

"What?" Yolo giggled in a tiny pair of shorts and half shirt. "This is what kids my age wear."

"It's cute," Casper interjected. "Ain't she cute Baron?"

The Baron shot her a quick glance, frowned, and turned away. He didn't particularly care for the girl. To keep it one hundred she scared him. Just like animals can see Angels and Jinn, the mute saw her evil.

"We're going to market, not spring break," Grimsly grumbled but acquiesced.

"Soooooo… can I kill the drug crew?" Yolo asked trying her luck once more.

"How would you do it? All four must go. We'll be hunting these guys for weeks, months, once the killing begins."

"Why don't I just lure them all to one place and kill 'em?" Yolo asked simply.

"Lure them all to one place?" Grimsly laughed dubiously. "You make it sound so simple. Just lure them all to one place."

"Pull over!" Yolo snapped, feeling salty from the snub.

"Excuse me?" he asked in wonderment. This was not the part of town where one just pulls over.

"Right there at the store, where those guys are. Pull over," she insisted. Mr. Grimsly sighed and complied pulling into the convenience store parking lot.

"I'll be right back," she said and hopped out. There was too much movement in the tiny shorts so Grimsly turned away.

The guys didn't. They cut their conversation and locked on to the sexy young thing. Their eyes shot from her thighs, crotch, stomach, and breasts then face as she approached. Grimsly watched as she giggled and flirted. A few seconds later, she led the fellows to the car.

"Mr. Grimsly these nice guys wanna try out the D.C. 2000," she said sweetly.

"Do they know it will take their heads off?" he asked.

"Yes. Don't you guys?"

"Yeah, that's cool. No problem." They all nodded in agreement. They left out the sex she promised in return.

"This takes off heads too," Grimsly barked producing a large revolver. The boys took flight, scattering in different direction.

"Told you," Yolo giggled as she got back in the car.

56

Yolo

The debate went back and forth to and from the market. They were still going at it when they reached the den with Casper and the Baron.

"Ok, ok. Just bait. No killing!" Grimsly said in defeat. He should have known that by that age there was no winning with a woman. As much as he hated to admit it, Yolo was a young woman.

"Thank you, Thank you!" she cheered and clapped. She ran over to hug her mentor and planted a grateful kiss on his cheek.

"You lure them to the Motor Lodge on 109 and I'll do the rest."

****

"I'm ready to change my mind," Mr. Grimsly pouted when Yolo click-clacked her heels into the den.

"What? I'm bait, boy bait," she giggled and did a spin in the tiny dress that caused the three men in the room to snap their heads away. Yolo got another giggle at their embarrassment. "So, I get to drive my car by myself today?"

"I guess," Grimsly sighed, like any father or father figure it was hard watching a girl become a woman. He had given her a convertible Camaro from an ex-employee who didn't need it anymore. Besides, the guy couldn't drive now anyway. Not in all the pieces, he was cut into. That's the thing about driving a car, you need feet and arms and a head…

"Thank you, thank you," Yolo sang and hopped around causing Casper, The Baron, and Grimsly to turn away again as her girl parts jiggled.

"Here, for protection only. Do...not, I repeat NOT...Shoot anyone," Grimsly instructed and handed her a pistol.

"No shooting," she vowed crossing her little black heart. She spun on her high heels and sashayed out of the room.

"You know that girl really is ready," Casper offered gently. He knew how close they were so he made sure to tread lightly.

"I know, more than ready actually. That's what I fear for her most, overkill."

Chapter 8

The drive from opulent Dix Hills to Amityville was like treading through time. When she arrived at the park any and everyone who was or wanted to be someone was in attendance.

Not only was Treble and company holding court under one of the pavilions but their baby mommas as well. The well-used ratchet girls had an adjacent pavilion to keep tabs on their investments. Having kids by dope boys was better than welfare. They were all on welfare too but welfare doesn't break you off with cash, drugs, and late night dick.

Shontay had two kids by Treble, which made her the leader; Alexis had babies by Ray, Reggie, and Ray. Kenya had two kids by Ace and Kim had kids by Reggie and Treble. Everyone pretended that her son didn't look just like Treble to spare their leader.

Amityville's booming drug trade meant everyone in attendances was fly. All the latest fashions were present along with the hottest wheels all waxed and shiny. Yolo pulled the drop top between two others and got out. Those closest to her got a great show of her bald vagina as she stepped out of the car.

"A-yo who the fuck is this bitch?" both Treble and Shontay wondered aloud as Yolo made her way through the park. She had already spotted her target and made a zigzag beeline towards them.

"That bitch ain't from here," Ray surmised since he never saw her before. "Probably Wyandanch or Brentwood?"

"That bitch ain't from here," Alexis said growing concerned. The new girl represented new pussy and guys love new pussy. For that reason, old pussy hates new pussy.

"Uh-oh! Look where she heading!" Kim groaned painfully.

"Oh no she not!" Shontay said seeing her heading towards her man. "Come on!"

Treble stood up so he could stand out. He did too in a crispy white wife beater that showed off his county jail push-ups. Typical upper torso nigga with pecs and abs but bird legs and chicken feet.

"Sup ma," Treble asked pulling Yolo next to him. He put a hand on her waist to feel her up and feel her out. If a strange girl lets you touch, she'll let you fuck.

"What's up is your hand is on me," Yolo replied with fake disgust. This was the first time a guy had touched her since puberty and her body reacted to it. She could feel a puddle forming between her legs. She hoped it wouldn't run down her leg since she wasn't wearing any panties.

"Just tryna talk to you lil mama," he said raising his hands in surrender. The high-pitched voice was so irritating she entertained the thought of shooting him in his throat.

"Well I can talk, I ain't made of braille, and you obviously ain't blind," she said placing a hand on his chest.

"That bitch just tried you!" Kenya protested. That was all it took to set it off.

"Bitch!" Shontay shrieked as she slapped Yolo from behind. Kenya and Alexis both got licks in while Kim watched.

Yolo's first instinct was to pull the pistol from her purse and murder everything moving. She knew if she did, she would have failed her mission. Her first mission and no telling when her mentor would give her another chance. Instead, she played girly and covered up to deflect the blows.

"Y'all buggin yo! Shantay! Alexis, Kenya, Kim!" he shouted as his boys pulled them off the girl.

Yolo recorded all the names then took mental snapshots of the faces once the fray was broken up. Ace had both Alexis and Shontay suspended in the air by their waists. They kicked and clawed at the air still trying to get to her. Meanwhile Ray and Reggie held back Kenya.

"Thank you, what was that all about?" Yolo whined slipping back into character. She pretended to be terrified as the attackers were pushed away. Part of being a killer is acting and girlfriend was killing it.

"Um, I don't know," Treble lied. "I don't know them hoes."

"How can I make it up to you?" she asked licking her lips.

"Just hit me so I can hit you," Treble laughed and scribbled his number.

"Why don't all of us hang out? I have some girlfriends! You guys don't mind white and Latino girls do you?"

"Don't mind at all!" No! No problem!" Ace, Ray and Reggie assured her. Treble too, he wanted a white or Latino too!

"Ok, meet us at the Motor Lodge on 109. Tomorrow night at... say ten?" Yolo pleaded batting her eyes. Knowing they wouldn't say no she didn't wait for an answer, she turned and gave a going away party by tossing her little ass from side to side, as she walked back to her car. Again, those closest to the Camaro got a shot of her vagina when she got back into her car and drove away.

****

"Well how'd it go young lady?" Grimsly asked as Yolo entered his room.

"Great. They'll be ready to die at ten pm sharp. Don't keep them waiting," she replied proudly. He offered a quick smile that changed to a pained expression. "What's wrong?"

"Nothing, I um...who are you again?" Grimsly asked. Yolo thought he was joking until half of his face suddenly drooped.

"Casper! Casper! Casper, Bar..." Yolo screamed as she ran for help. She gave up calling the useless Baron. All he was good for was decoration.

"What? What's wrong?" Casper asked looking terrified as he answered the call. Yolo saw fear in his eyes but was too young to understand it.

"It's Mr. Grimsly! Something is wrong!" she shouted, snatched his hand, and dragged him to his room.

"Oh no! A stroke," Casper sighed recognizing the signs immediately.

"I'll call 911," Yolo said rushing for the landline. She was now terrified herself at the deadly diagnosis. This was the first man in her life who loved her and she loved in return.

The three men of the house were the only ones who didn't come at her dick first. No wonder she developed a hatred of dicks.

"Call 911? Here?" Casper asked at the absurdity of the statement. Even the Baron raised an eyebrow at the statement. "I'll call the private doctor."

The private doctor was a fifty something white man with an annoying chuckle and roaming eyes. He felt Yolo and down with his eyes before even glancing over at the patient.

"Him, not me!" Yolo said dangerously and pointed at Grimsly.

"Ah yes, let's see," he said as he went to examine him. "It's a stroke alright."

Poor Grimsly was now completely paralyzed unable to move or speak. Even worse, he was complete alert, trapped inside his own body. All he could do was look and blink. Every time he caught Yolo's eyes, he blinked rapidly. Only it was too much for her so she turned away. The doctor hooked up monitors and a feeding tube before packing his equipment.

"How long is he going be like that?" Yolo asked sadly.

"Not long," the doctor laughed. Yolo smiled along with him suddenly optimistic.

"So he'll get better?" she cheered.

"Oh no, he's dead," he laughed again sending her into one of her white-hot fits of rage.

"Is this the only doctor you have?" Yolo growled to Casper.

"No, I have a cou…" was all he got out before Yolo pulled her gun and fired into the doctor's smirk. That shut up the chuckling. He sure didn't find that funny.

Baron cringed at the explosion of violence while Casper laughed Mr. Grimsly was quite amused as well but couldn't show it. Instead, he just blinked approvingly.

"Guess I'll call the cleaner to come scrape him up. Better call in another hitter to handle that Amityville situation as well," he said. Casper laughed internally thinking, Wait for it…

"No! I can handle it! Amityville I mean. I'm not touching him," she said turning her nose up at the dead doctor.

"Four guys? All dead? No trace? No witnesses?" Casper dared while Grimsly blinked 'no'.

"Hells yeah! I already got them to meet me at ten. Come ten fifteen them fuckas is dead!" she assured him. She left out the part about killing their baby mommas. That was personal after all. This was business.

"Handle it then," Casper shrugged and walked out.

Yolo sat with Grimsly as the cleaner came and took the doctor away. He was headed either to the dump or to feed the pigs but she didn't ask. Didn't care, she just sat and watched her surrogate father blink until he fell asleep.

Chapter 9

"Yo we gon' switch on these hoes!" As soon as I fuck this bitch y'all can heave her!" Treble proclaimed. New pussy is exciting enough on its own but white and Latino pussy is exotic. Like driving a foreign car or eating strange food. "Bet!" Ace, Reggie and Ray agreed. They were all down for the gangbang. They sat around the motel room sipping, smoking, and watching porn to get ready. Dudes always put on a porn with a good sloppy blowjob as a hint. Or constantly write about them; hint.

"They're here!" Reggie shouted and jumped to his feet. He rushed over and snatched the door open with a bulge in his pants from the movie. He smiled at Yolo then looked past her for the white and Latino girls. "Where are your friends?"

"They coming, stuck in traffic," she replied and stepped inside. She ran her eyes around the room and saw everyone was accounted for. "I brought bubbly!"

"I'll take that. What's up girl?" Treble said rushing forward. He licked his lips trying to be sexy but still sounded like a bitch without any bass in his voice.

As Treble pulled the cork out Yolo pulled plastic flutes from the bag. Treble was too thirsty to notice the cork came out too easily minus the pop that makes popping bottles fun. He filled his friends' glasses and saw Yolo didn't have one.

"You not drinking ma?" he wondered.

"Oh no. That stuff is poison!" she giggled wickedly at her own inside joke. The men didn't get it but I bet you did.

Suddenly the action on the TV caught her attention. On screen was a very pretty, young light-skinned girl sucking a long black dick. There were enough curvy veins in it to be a short story in braille. The girl was working it too; all lips, wrist and neck. Yolo was mesmerized.

"Come on lil mama," Treble said pulling Yolo onto his lap as they all watched the show.

"Son blinking his eyes like he bout to pass the fuck out!" Ray cheered. Good head does deserve a cheer.

"Nah, he sending Morse code! He saying damn this bitch got some good ass head!" Reggie laughed.

"Morse code!" Yolo jumped up and shouted. She finally realized that's what Grimsly had been doing. She wanted to just shoot them now and rush home to see what he was saying. In the end, she decided to wait. It wouldn't be long anyway.

"Chill baby," Treble said pulling her back on his lap. To help her chill he slid a finger past her wet panties and fondled her clit.

"No!" Yolo shouted when he tried to push the digit inside of her. She clamped her thighs and grabbed his wrist to prevent the penetration.

"Ok ma, chill," he relented and went back to making circles on her clit.

Treble played in her pussy with one hand while sipping champagne with the other. Yolo was nearing the first orgasm of her life when a deep yawn interrupted him. Yawns are contagious in general but especially when everyone has been poisoned. She smiled brightly as the men all yawned and fell over. Treble took one last deep breath and exhaled his soul.

Yolo was too curious about what was happening between her legs to ignore it. She put her finger where Treble's finger had been and did what he did. A minute later, her whole body convulsed when she came.

"Dayum!" Yolo exclaimed at the life changing moment. She picked up the smoldering blunt from the ashtray and took a pull. She mimicked what she saw Ray do and let the smoke billow out her mouth while inhaling into her nostrils.

"Eww! Why you gotta be all nasty with it?" Yolo grimaced when the male porn actor pulled his dick out and skeeted on the pretty face. "Ok, time to get back to work."

Yolo slipped on latex gloves and collected evidence like a CSI tech. She checked each pulse as she took the plastic glasses back. She flushed the blunt clip with her DNA and prepared to leave. Once she hit the door, she doubled back and took all of their phones. This would make tracking the girls down that much easier. This wasn't business. This was personal.

****

"Well how did it go?" Casper asked when Yolo returned. Her making it back was good but four dead guys would be even better,

"Told you I got this homie!" she shouted back twisting her lips and cocking her head back confidently. She lifted her

Sa'id Salaam

hand for a high five and got it. She tried her lick with the Baron and got the usual. Nothing.

"Ok then," Yolo giggled at the snub and then got serious. "Oh I know why Mr. Grimsly keeps blinking! It's Morse code!"

"Yes! Damn why didn't I think of that?" Casper asked popping his own forehead. As if, he could have had a V-8. "How did you figure it out?"

"Um..." Yolo stammered remembering the porno tape. "Come on let's go see what he's trying to say!"

"You know Morse code?" he asked as he followed her to Mr. Grimsly's room.

"No, I'll Google it" she replied and rushed into his room. He blinked, 'How dare you barge in without knocking,' but she wasn't ready yet. After a brief YouTube video and instructions from professor Google she was all set.

"Now say what you were saying. Go slow and take your time," Yolo said loudly as if he were hearing impaired instead of paralyzed. She began to translate the dots and dashes as he blinked. A dark cloud came over her face as she read the words.

"No!" Yolo stood and yelled like a truculent child.

"What?" Casper asked about the sudden outburst. Yolo refused to reply so he took the paper from her hand and read. 'K-I-L-L M-E'

"But....why?" Casper frowned. He gave the paper back so Yolo could translate what came next.

68

'D-O-N-T L-E-A-V-E M-E L-I-K-E T-H-I-S K-I-L-L M-E P-L-E-A-S-E,' Yolo read along shaking her head.

"He's right you know. He's a proud man and deserves better than this," Casper said softly. Grimsly seemed to nod his eyelids in agreement.

"I know," Yolo sighed. Casper was right. He did deserve not to live like this. "I can't."

"I'll call another doctor," he said and walked out of the room to do just that.

"You're welcome," she said in response to the next message he blinked at her. They shared one final conversation until the doctor arrived.

"What is that?" Yolo asked the balding black man as he filled a syringe with clear liquid from a vial.

"It's a sedative. Don't worry; he won't feel any pain. He'll just go to sleep and won't wake up until judgment day," he said softly.

"I love you too," Yolo smiled in return to Mr. Grimsly's final words. It was the first time he ever said it but she knew it all along. No one ever treated her kindly until he came along. All kindness and compassion died along with him.

The death rattle alerted them that Mr. Grimsly had left the building. The doctor leaned over to close his eyes while Yolo re-filled the syringe.

"Ouch! What are you doing?" the man asked after Yolo stuck him with the needle.

"Don't worry, you won't feel any pain. Just go to sleep and wake up on judgment day," she teased. The heavy sedative worked quickly and soon there were two dead men in the room.

"What the hell did you do?" Casper demanded when he led the cleaner in the room to collect his mentor.

"He killed Grimsly so..." Yolo grumbled.

"So I'm running out of doctors is so!" he shot back.

"No pigs!" Yolo growled at the cleaner.

"No, no pigs," he assured her. He walked over to the man he known for many murders over many years and removed his hat. He said a silent prayer before crossing himself and got to work.

With Grimsly died restraint. The murderer with morals kept Casper in check more often than not. There were times when the boss ordered whole families hit but had to settle for one or two deaths. Murder makes a statement and the more heinous it is, is an exclamation point. He knew Yolo wouldn't mind going the extra mile. In fact, he planned to encourage her to go there.

Chapter 10

Casper waited until he heard Yolo enter the den before he hit the play button. At first, she thought the footage of the girl fight was from the internet until she recognized herself.

"Hey that's me! Where did you get that?" she demanded of the footage of Shontay and company jumping on her.

"Black Mob?" he replied sarcastically. "My question for you is what are you going to do about it?"

"I'm going to each one of their houses and I'm going to kill anything alive. People, pets, plants, whatever it is, it's dying," Yolo vowed. She planned to sneak and carry out the attacks but the nod of Casper's smiling head was a green light.

"Have fun," he said to her back as she rushed happily from the room. The Baron twisted his lip like he wanted to protest but said nothing.

"That's what I thought you'd say; why don't I call for some strippers? Order some wings and blowjobs?"

The Baron still didn't reply but wouldn't have said no anyway. The large man was very fond of wings and blowjobs just like every guy.

****

Kenya and Alexis planned to make killing them as easy as possible. Half of Amityville was in hiding after the quadruple homicide but not these two. No, they wanted to hangout, smoke weed, and drink beer like always. Usually it cost a little head or a little ass but tonight it would cost them a little more. Actually a lot more.

As soon as Yolo pulled on the block, she spotted her targets. She doubled checked their pictures not believing how easy this would be. They left the weed spot and hit the corner store. While Kenya paid for cigars with change, Alexis swiped a forty of malt liquor. Ironically, their next stop was the scene of the crime. Call it fate, karma, whatever, but they were about to die at the same place they transgressed.

The park was off limits to cars after sunset. It used to be the place to park and fuck in cars but the police started shaking them down. If you walked in you could fuck or drink or smoke under one of the pavilions.

Yolo got to use her stalking skills in real life. No more practice, she was hunting for real. She parked a few blocks away and circled around to sneak up on her prey. She crept up using the loudmouth girls' loud conversation as cover.

"Man that's fucked up Ray is dead," Kenya griped bitterly. "Now I gotta have some more damn kids by one of these niggas!"

"I know right! They got all my baby daddies at one time! Coulda at least left me one," Alexis groaned. Luckily, most of Ace's possessions were in her name. Unluckily Yolo was there.

Yolo lifted the 40 caliber to the back of Kenya's head at the same time she lifted the beer to her mouth. At the same time, the frothy fluid hit her tongue, Yolo fired. The slug easily passed through her unused brain, out her mouth, and through the bottle. It would technically qualify as a trick shot had it been a competition. It wasn't though.

"Aww man look what you did to my beer! Look at my friend!" Alexis complained in order of importance. She was about to day some more dumb shit until she recognized the face. "You!"

"Me," Yolo laughed waving her hand amicably. The wave was friendly but the smoking canon in the other hand not so much.

"Girl I know you ain't trippin' 'bout that little shit last week. Here girl," Alexis said and passed the blunt. You gotta give the girl credit; she was tryin' to stay alive.

"Um...ok?" Yolo said accepting the weed. The girl was nice and the weed smelled good so why not? Yolo was still going to kill her.

"Oh I like your hair! I'ma go natural too one day. Gon' have to cut all this perm out first," Alexis admired.

"I've never had a perm my whole life," Yolo said proudly. Luckily, she murdered She-Ra before she got a chance to fry her head.

They made girly small talk as they passed the blunt back and forth as if Kenya wasn't at their feet leaking brain matter. The moment of truth came when the weed came to an end. Alexis stood up and tried her luck.

"Welp, nice seeing you again. I'm 'bout to go," she said and turned to leave.

"Ok bye!" Yolo sang, and then shot her in the back of her head too. "Two down, two to go."

****

Kim was a little harder to kill because she barely left the house. When she did, it was always in the middle of the day with her kids in tow. Reggie left a few pounds of weed at her house, which kept her from the weed spot. Yolo had staked out the spot but never saw her. Shontay on the other hand must have been suffering from glaucoma or cancer or something because she was there five times a day, every day. Yolo could have gotten her several times over but didn't. She was saving her for last. She had something special in store for her.

Since she spent so much time stalking the weed spot, Yolo ventured in and brought a bag. She made a mess in the car trying to roll a smoke-able blunt and got it five tries later. After blazing, she was high and hungry. There was a Chinese restaurant on the block so she took a break and went in.

"Cat fried rice in lobster sauce and an egg roll," Yolo demanded and cracked up at her own joke.

"Um...we no sell cat," the Chinese lady said looking guilty. With her lying ass, that's all they served was cat. It didn't matter if you ordered chicken, beef, or pork fried rice, your ass was getting cat. "Shri fri ri wi robster sauce?" she offered instead and Yolo cracked up again.

A phone rang and the woman turned to answer. Yolo only half listened to the delivery order until she heard a familiar address. "12 Rawrence Street. Ten mini"

Yolo quickly got her order and took off. It was time for a special delivery.

"Who!" Kim barked from behind her triple locked door.

Yolo

"You order chini foo?" Yolo called out and covered her mouth from giggling again.

"Bout damn time!" Kim barked and snatched the door open. She didn't even bother to look as she turned to get her purse. Her children were all in the living room engrossed in play. Treble's son was on the game console while Reggie's two daughters had a tea party. Yolo pulled a gun.

Kim turned and looked right down the barrel of the gun. In it, her whole life flashed before her eyes. She could only shake her head at all the poor choices and bad decisions she'd made. Three were staring up at her now.

"What about my kids?" she pleaded. Just like a sorry ass baby momma trying to use her kids against a man. It didn't work then and it didn't work now. Yolo fired off three quick shots killing each child in their spot.

"What kids?" she asked with a shrug.

"I ain't even touch you, I didn't hit you," Kim pleaded.

"I know but see, there's this guy named Killa," Yolo said sounding like a teen with a crush. Mainly because she was a teen with a crush.

"I don't even know if he's real or not but legend has it that he killed one hundred people before he turned 21 and I'm tryna do the same and I got a long way to go cuz right now I only got um, let's see... ok Jane, Larry. She-Ra, Mr. Wheeler cuz he tried to fuck me and I don't play that, um, of course, you know Treble, Ace, Reggie, and Ray. That sounds like a singing group don't it? Anyway, a doctor, no two doctors,

Alexis, Kenya, your kids, and you!" Yolo rambled and then fired. "16 down, 84 to go."

****

"Shontay Mo'nay Jackson?" the uniformed officer asked formally; when Shontay finally pulled the door open. Had she not seen the uniform and badge the door would not have been opened. Even though she was relieved to see the cop, she still paused to recall any open charges or missed court dates.

"I'm Shontay Mo'nay Jackson," she replied when nothing came to mind.

"Miss Jackson you are in extreme danger. As you are aware, someone has murdered several of your friends, we have reason to believe they may target you as well," he detailed.

"Several of my friends, someone killed all of my friends! They even killed Kim's kids! I got kids," Shontay moaned pointing at the toddler toddling around and infant sleeping on the sofa.

"We need to get you to a safe house until this thing is over."

"Ok, let me pack!" Shontay said and turned to do just that.

"No time, everything you'll need is at the house, we must leave now," the cop urged.

Shontay scooped the baby up and grabbed her diaper bag. The toddler followed her as she followed the police to the unmarked car.

"You mind if I smoke?" she asked as soon as they merged onto the Long Island Expressway. It sounded like a question but she'd already pulled a blunt from her purse and pushed in the car lighter.

"Won't your kids mind?" the officer winced from the display of piss poor parenting.

"Nah they used to it," she replied and sparked the blunt. She took a big pull and filled the car with funk from the skunk weed. The vibration of the car and weed smoke put the kids to sleep.

"So…y'all figured out who is doing this?" she asked between tokes.

"Oh we know exactly who is responsible for the murders. She is a very dangerous young woman," he replied with a nod.

"She! A woman killed all my friends? Babies too?" Shontay screamed causing her kids to stir.

"Like I said, she's a very dangerous person," the cop repeated.

"Where we going anyway?" she asked halfway through Jersey.

"Pennsylvania, relax, we still have a little way to go," he answered. Shontay wasted no time in joining her children in dreamland.

****

"We're here," the police officer announced loud enough to awaken Shontay. He pulled off the main road onto a dirt driveway leading into the woods. A hundred feet later, he had to get out and unlock a very secure gate. Another hundred feet they pulled to a stop in front of a modern log cabin.

"Stink mommy," the toddler proclaimed, wrinkling her little face up.

"It do! How you gon' bring us somewhere that stink like this!" Shontay asked hotly.

"Don't worry; you won't be here long at all. Promise," he said unlocking the doors. "Go on inside, they're waiting on you."

"Oh ok, well thank you officer...I didn't get your name," Shantay asked from outside the car.

"Just call me Casper," he replied and pulled away. Shontay shrugged at the odd name and walked to the cabin's door. When she knocked, it eased open.

"Hello? Anyone here? I'm bout to smoke a blunt," she called out as she stepped into the sparse front room.

"In here!" a female voice from another room said, so Shontay followed it. When she found it, she got the shock of her life. At least it would be the last shock of her life.

"You!" Shontay shouted at the large pistol laying on the table in front of Yolo.

"Hey girl," Yolo sang as if they were best fucking friends. As if, her and her girlfriends hadn't jumped her, as if she wasn't about to murder her. "Have a seat."

"What is this place?" Shontay asked looking at the morticians table in the kitchen. She sat the baby carrier down and sat as ordered.

"Cuff your wrists. It makes it easier," Yolo demanded pointing at the cuff attached to the arms of the armchair.

"You ain't gon' kill me in front of my children are you?" Shontay pleaded clicking one cuff on her wrist then the next.

"Oh no. I wouldn't do that! You have my word," she said and stood. Yolo put the gun on the table and opened the back door. The pigs went crazy thinking it was time to eat. They were right. Yolo plucked the baby up and tossed his little ass right in the middle of the pen. One bold hog stole a bite before the head hog grabbed it and retreated to his corner. Shontay was so shocked it took her a few seconds to register what just happened. When Yolo picked her daughter up, she figured it out real quick.

"No!" Shontay howled as her first-born sailed into the back yard. She landed with a thud and was pounced upon instantly. The hungry hogs took her apart so quickly the child hardly got a chance to scream. Two kids were hardly enough to satisfy the beasts. Luckily, more was on the way.

"Man that's fucked up," Shontay muttered in defeat. No way was she getting through this alive and she accepted it.

"No what was fucked up was you jumping me. If you never touched me this wouldn't be happening," Yolo explained. As she spoke, she tilted a bottle onto a cloth. Shontay asked about it with her eyebrows so Yolo explained. "Chloroform. It'll help you sleep while I prep you."

"Prep me wha…" she tried to ask but had her mouth and nostrils covered before she could get it out. She was asleep in seconds but she would have her answer soon enough.

"Hey sleepy head," Yolo sang when Shontay blinked awake.

"Huh?" Shontay wondered. Wondered why she was strapped to the morgue table. Wondered why she could barely feel her legs. Wondered why they both wore earplugs and wondered what was next.

"I gave you an epidural. It's my first one so I hope it worked," Yolo said and cut her left foot off.

"Oooyeee!" she screamed her reply. "I feel it!"

"My bad," Yolo said verbally although her shoulder shrug translated to 'oh well.' She tossed the foot out the back door.

"How crazy is it to feed people's feet to pigs? You know cuz people eat pigs' feet, well not me cuz that's nasty but I'm just saying."

"Eeoowee!" Shontay screamed cutting her off, Guess it was fair since Yolo was cutting her off. She could only watch as the other foot went out the door.

Luckily, for Shontay, she bled to death halfway through the first leg. Yolo took the girl apart just like a chicken. And just like a chicken, she fed her to the hogs. She found the blunt in the girls' purse and lit it.

"83," Yolo said blowing a smoke ring and watching it waft towards the ceiling.

Chapter 11

Yolo turned 17 with 25 bodies under her belt and 75 left to meet her twisted goals. By 18, the stunning beauty was at an even 30 and beginning to get depressed, thinking she may not make it. Luckily, for her niggas kept fucking up as if they wanted to donate their life to help her meet her quota.

"Great news!" Casper cheered finding Yolo in the den. As usual, she was online reading reports and rumors regarding her favorite mass murderer.

"Yesss!" Yolo cheered pumping her little fist. Casper always referred to an impending murder as good news so she knew so she knew somebody had to die.

"Oh and I want it to be messy. It's time to send a message."

"Regular messy or urban fiction author hating on each other messy?" she asked hoping for the latter.

"Urban fiction. Cut throat, slimy, backstabbing, screen shot, grown ass men acting like high-school girls, in-box gossip messy!" he stressed rubbing his hands together in eager anticipation.

"How many?" Yolo asked twisting her face into a 'what you talkin 'bout Willis.' She never asked why because she couldn't possibly care less. All she wanted was bodies to add to her death toll. Isn't it great when young people set goals? Maybe not in this sense but in general, yeah.

"Just one. An apostate, low life traitor," Casper replied of the bad Reverend James.

Ol' Rev started off on the right foot, preaching and pastoring real good. As a result, the church grew along with his fame and fortune. As a result of that the good church ladies starting throwing that good church lady pussy at him. He was getting so much ass he started peddling it throughout the congregation. It grew and grew until he had a full-fledged pimping operation going. That's the thing about good pussy; it cannot be contained.

Only problem was that Memphis was a Black Mob city. Once Casper got wind of the pimpin' pastor, he put the squeeze on him. He got a whiff of that southern vagina and sent an Emissary.

"You can't pimp a pimp!" Reverend James said sounding just like a pimp. He smoothed his perm back with a diamond-crusted hand and stomped his gator boot as he spoke.

"Fine," Mr. Grimsly said and prepared to leave. Not without screwing a long silencer on his pistol to kill him first. A loaded gun is a great negotiation tool and the negotiations began.

"I'm just saying 40% is a bit high," Rev suggested but Grimsly kept on screwing. He wasn't sent to make deals, that's not what he did. Rev was smart enough to pick up on that. "You know what? Once you say it out loud, it don't sound so bad. 40% it is!"

"It does have a nice ring to it," Grimsly agreed and began to unscrew the silencer.

Ol' Rev did good for a while with the payments. Every now and then, he would slack off and Grimsly would come for lunch. No threats, just fine southern fare with a pistol on the table. Once there was no more Grimsly, there were no more payments. He didn't know about Yolo yet. He was about to find out.

As usual, Yolo did her homework on her target. She learned his movements, hangouts, and habits. Learned pastor was a freak too. Liked putting things in women's asses as much as he liked them putting things in his ass. He liked to fuck but wanted to get fucked in return, with his nasty ass. He also had a thing for young girls. Unfortunately, Yolo was a young girl and she planned to fuck him.

Reverend James mounted his pulpit and began to preach. Ironically, the sermon was about morality. About being chaste and upright until he spotted Yolo. There she was on the front row with her natural hair pulled into a wavy ponytail. She had on her Sunday best minus panties. When she had his attention she popped her legs open long enough for him to see the pretty kitty. A nice bald pussycat.

"Shit!" Rev cursed at the sight of the plumpness staring back at him.

"Bullshit!" his assistant preacher/hype man cosigned.

"That's right! Pastor said shit cuz that's what it is!" he said to the stunned faces. The bare box stole his train of thought as vagina has a tendency to do. He freestyled the rest of the sermon and lead the congregation in a brief prayer.

The second he 'amenned' he made a beeline over to Yolo.

"Nice sermon pastor sir," Yolo offered shyly. Part of being a good killer is being a good actor. It was easy for her to play virginal since she really was a virgin.

"Thank you chile, you must be new 'round here?" he replied staring at her nipples through the dress.

"I'm is. I just moved from Mississippi to stay with my grandma but she put me out," she pouted helplessly.

"Sho-nuff?" he said scheming already. If she had nowhere to go, she was as good as fucked. "Why in the world would she put a precious young thing like you out?"

"Caught me sucking her husband thang. He won't my grandpa though," she said lowering her head in shame. The man's knees buckled slightly and his vision went blurry from the sudden erection.

"Did, di, did you swallow?" He had to know.

"Of course. I'm 'posed to ain't I?" Yolo asked innocently. The preacher had heard enough. He snatched her by her thin waist and rushed her from the church.

"Ravened James?" several people called after him as he blew off all of his after church meetings. Whatever they wanted would have to wait, pastor was trying to get laid. He was about to get laid alright.

"Where we going?" Yolo asked as downtown Memphis sped by the luxury car's window.

"The church keeps a few apartments for the hoes…eh, I mean homeless women. Get 'em off the streets, help 'em earn they keep," he replied. He left out the part about selling pussy to earn your keep.

Yolo

The girl was so fresh and clean he decided he'd keep her as a personal sidepiece for a while. At least until something else fresh and clean came along. That's when he would put that ass for sale. Well, for rent actually, since no one really buys the pussy. Well, married men, but that's another story.

"This is nice," Yolo marveled at the cute apartment. If she wasn't living in a large mansion, she might want one just like it. It had nice furniture and all the latest electronics.

"Thank you," the preacher replied as if the church money hadn't paid for it. This was no time for show and tell; he was ready to get his dick sucked and butt plugged.

"Let me show you the bedroom," he suggested and pulled her towards it.

"This is ni... oh!" Yolo exclaimed when he shoved her on to the bed. She almost pulled the pistol from her purse until pastor dove tongue first under her dress. When she felt his mouth on her box, she finished her sentence, "Nice."

Yolo tried to stay professional but the good tongue-lashing turned her into a girl. She tossed her head, 'oohing', and 'aahing' until she 'arghed!' and erupted. The rev was an expert pussy eater and clamped his lips on hers to suck all the juice out the box. Would have sucked it inside out if she hadn't stopped him.

"Ok, my turn," Yolo said prying his mouth off her vagina. She rolled off the bed and watched his strip so fast superman would have said 'dayum!'

Rev produced a nice thick erection that made Yolo glad she wasn't having sex with the man. She meanwhile pulled out

85

the specially designed dildo. It was so large she wondered if it would even fit. He took one look at it and hopped on the bed. He was doggy style with an arch in his back eager to get fucked. With his nasty ass. Yolo shrugged and went over to try it.

"Mmm, give it to me," Pastor moaned as he was penetrated.

Yolo scrunched her face up in disgust as the device went in so easily. Almost as if, his ass had suction. She barely had time to turn it on before it disappeared from sight.

"Oh yes! What's that?" he gushed delightfully when it began buzzing inside of him.

"That," Yolo began as she backed away out of blast range, "is a shape charge filled with buckshot. You really have to be careful about what you let people put in your ass you know."

The preacher frowned as he tried to process the words she spoke. It sounded dangerous but the vibrations felt wonderful. Had he had more time minus the distraction he would have figured it out. Only time was a luxury he didn't have. The twenty second timer ran its course and the device detonated.

A muffled explosion sent the buckshot into the man's body. It ripped his internal organs to shreds killing him almost instantly. He tried to speak but his damaged lungs wouldn't take in air. Instead, he closed his eyes and went to hell. It was messy just like ordered.

Chapter 12

As fun as killing the preacher may have been it was still only one man. Yolo was delighted when Casper told her about the next job. Most of the jobs were business related but this one was personal. This one was pay back and Casper wanted a front row seat.

"Hey! Look it who it is!" Vito shouted as Casper walked into the Brighton Beach bar. There are plenty of bars in the Italian section of Brooklyn but this particular watering hole was the hang out of his old crew. This is where they came to unwind after a long day of mob activities.

"The one and only!" Casper exclaimed happily. Truth be told, the only reason he was happy to see them all together was so they could die, all together. He eagerly accepted each outstretched hand and man hug.

First was Guido since they were family. Cousins on their father's side. That blood relation didn't stop him a millisecond from snitching on the man. Even though Casper had nothing to do with the illegal pill mill he ran, he put all the blame on him when the feds came knocking.

"Good to see you cuz," Guido said embracing him. "Where you laying ya head dese days?"

"Good to see you too. I got a little shack out on Long Island. Nothing fancy," Casper replied referring to the mansion.

"Pizan!" Joey cheered throwing his short stubby arms open. He had an amateur cocaine ring that he too blamed on Casper.

"Look at you! Round as ever!" he said accepting the hug.

Next were Pauly and Vito who also pinned their crimes on the outsider once they got pinched. The four made men knew they would be killed for violating the Mob's no drug policy. Since the half-Irish Casper could never be a full member, they sold him out.

The bosses were ready to snuff him out like a cigarette butt had he said one word. Even his friends were shocked when he kept it real, and kept quiet. He never got caught for his own operation but was going to prison anyway. It would have been crazy going to trial with that many fingers pointed at him. Instead, he took it on the chin, which led to him taking it up the ass.

His first night in the big house was spent with a big black guy inside of him. The Baron saved his butt hole from further abuse and Casper vowed to take care of him for life. He made the large mute the face of his Black Mob and the rest was underworld history.

Only fools forgive and forget. Casper was no fool and wanted revenge. He dreamed of it nightly until it consumed him. That day was the day, judgment day Italian style.

"Drinks on me!" Casper announced setting off a round of applause at the first round of drinks. The bar had just emptied when the bartender Ray, brought over a bottle of cognac.

Yolo

"So what youse got going these days?" Pauly asked halfway through the second round. Judging by his attire, watch, and generosity, Casper was getting to the money.

"Got me a small stable of whores. Just black and Latino cocksuckers," he replied setting out the bait.

"Good money in head?" Guido wanted to know. He should already know judging by how much money he spent on it.

"Eh, it's a living. Trick is volume; you gotta get 'em in, get 'em off, and keep it moving. I got this one black girl, natural born cocksucker! I swear she could come and get all of us off in ten minutes flat. Blow youse guys mind!"

The table fell silent at the threat of good head. Nothing goes with cognac like a good blowjob. As a matter of fact, head goes well with everything. Makes everything better, fishing, driving, watching a movie, surfing the net, writing a book...

"Call her up," Vito said making it sound more like a dare than a request.

"Yeah, hit her up. Get her over so we can see if it's as good as you say it is," Joey co-signed.

"Youse guys really ready to have your brains blown?" Casper asked to be sure. Murder is always better when they beg for it.

"Sure! Why not! Hells yeah! Run it!" came the replies from around the table. They begged for it.

"Ok let's see where she's at," Casper said reaching for his cell phone. He hit speed dial and got you know who on the line. "Where you at? I got some guys over here who desperately need their minds blown. Um huh...ok...great!"

"W...w...what she say?" Vito stammered eagerly.

"Youse guys are in luck, she leaving Brooklyn Heights now. She'll be here in a few," he announced setting off another round of cheers. No one noticed the fact that he didn't give directions. Not that he needed to since Yolo was right outside.

Yolo sat in the backseat of the car cyber-stalking Killa. She used Google Earth to take a virtual tour of the Bronx housing projects he grew up in. She planned to go make a pilgrimage there as soon as she got the nerve.

The nasty ass preacher was her first brush with sex and was nagging her. She could still feel his big tongue on her vagina weeks later. As a result, she played in her toy box daily. It was time to meet this Killa person and give him some pussy. She had been saving herself for him.

When she calculated enough time had passed to travel from the Heights to the beach Yolo prepared to go inside. Wasn't much of a preparation since all she did was put a sawed off shotgun in her bag.

"Someone ordered a blow job!" Yolo demanded as she stepped into the bar. She punctuated the question by standing wide legged with a hand on her hip.

"We sure did!" Ray replied. He rushed over to lock the door behind her so they would not be disturbed. He should have ran. Should have took off up the street and ran for his life.

"So who's first?" she barked.

"Me!" everyman shouted raising a hand. Except Casper that is. He knew what was coming and wanted no parts of it. Not to mention, she was family.

Vito jumped up but Pauly shoved him out of the way. Fat Joey was too slow and got up behind Guido. Pauly arrived first, dick in hand and was the first to die. Yolo whipped out the sawed off and blew his dick out of his hand. The bar shook from the roar of the shotgun.

Vito frowned at the gaping hole where his manhood once lived. He was about to cry but Yolo shot him in his neck nearly taking his head off. Pauly tried to run but another blast from the shotgun opened a hole big enough to see through.

Ray was about that action and tried to rush the girl. Yolo twisted her lips as if to say 'yeah right' and fired. The slug caught him in his kneecap and amputated it. She strolled over to finish him off.

"Oh, oh! You remember that movie 'Face Off'?" Yolo asked.

"Huh?" Ray frowned. He of course remembered the movie, that was a good ass movie but he wasn't in the mood to talk about it.

"Forget it then," she whined and took his face off with her next shot. "No sense of humor."

"Casper what the fuck!" Guido begged. "Make her stop!"

"Look it cuz, I know youse hot about us selling youse out," Joey guessed correctly. "I got a million dollars! Let me live and youse guys can have it!"

"Where the fuck you get a mil from?" Guido wanted to know. They had been partners for years and he was nowhere close to that number.

"I've been skimming from you fucks for years!" Joey laughed. "Cuzzo kill them cocksuckers and take the money!"

"I'll let Yolo decide. Let him live?

"Um…nah," Yolo giggled and fired. Joey's head exploded like a Gallagher trick.

"They would have killed us. The bosses, they would have killed our families," Guido explained. "We had no choice."

"There's always a choice. Yolo say good bye to Guido"

"Bye Guido," Yolo said and sent him bye-bye with a tug on the shotgun's trigger. They looked around at the carnage in the room and nodded in satisfaction.

"Have fun?" Casper asked as they hit the door.

"I did! Thank you," Yolo cheered happily then twisted her lips ruefully.

"What's wrong?" he asked seeing her lip poked out.

"That's only 36," she pouted as if she were about to cry.

"Well why don't you blow up their funeral? That'll get your number up a bit," Casper offered in consolation.

Of course, the lovely little lunatic agreed and did just that. She secured a bomb from the local bomb guy and planted it in the funeral home. When the joint funeral for the four close friends was held, she blew it up. The blast claimed twenty-five more lives bringing her death toll to a respectable 61. No too bad for a kid.

Chapter 13

"Nice!" Yolo sang as she looked at her reflection in the dentist's hand held mirror.

"Nice and dangerous. I can't believe I let you talk me into making those," the dentist lamented. He should believe it since he was greedy enough to do anything for money. That's why Yolo was in his chair now. His ass was in trouble.

The 'those' he spoke of was the platinum fangs he made for the girl. As the go to guy for hip-hop artists, he had fashioned plenty of them. Some had diamonds and rubies but none like these. These were fully functional with long dagger like canine and razor sharp incisors. Somebody could get hurt with those. Somebody was going to get hurt with those.

The dentist along with all Black Mob associates were forbidden from doing business with anyone on Casper's black list. Big Kodac was on the black list. The owner of Kodac records in Atlanta, GA was once a Black Mob drug dealer. He formed the record label as a front to launder dirty drug money. They signed one cornball rapper by the name of Nano just for show. The rap world obviously loves cornball, commercial crap as much as urban lit and he blew up.

Blew up so high that he was soon generating millions in revenue for Kodac records. Kodac figured that since it was rap and not crack money that he didn't have to pay. Figured wrong, dead wrong. He disappeared from sight knowing

Casper would kill him. That got him put on the black list that the dentist violated by making the rapper a grill.

Casper just happened to be channel surfing when he came across Nano doing an interview. He was amused by the illiterate little idiot's antics until he shouted out the dentist and made one of those grimaces to show off the platinum and diamond teeth. Casper was furious at being disobeyed.

"Yolo!" Casper screamed with just a hint of bitch in his voice. The Baron heard it too and smiled internally since he never smiled externally.

The Baron recalled hearing Casper scream like that when B.B. took his bagina in prison. Bagina is boy pussy if you ain't know. Casper heard it too and adjusted his voice down an octave to compensate.

"Yes?" Yolo asked rushing into the den hearing the tone she loved so much.

The Baron turned his head upon arrival of the scantily clad girl. Now that Grimsly was gone, she got to dress as sexy as she wanted to. Feeling safe around Casper and the Baron, she was almost always nearly nude at home.

"You see those pretty gold teeth?" Casper asked pointing to the paused image on the hundred-inch screen.

"Oh they are pretty! I want some!" she gushed like a girl.

"I want those. I want you to go down to Atlanta and pull every one of them out of his mouth and bring them to me!"

"Ok," Yolo sang as casually as if he asked for a glass of tea. She turned ready to go do just that right then.

"Wait! First, get you a set made from that traitor in Jamaica. Make it his last," Casper growled.

"Oh Jamaica! I can't wait! I'ma go on the beach and swimming and..."

"Uh...Jamaica Queens," Casper interjected.

"Oh, I knew that," Yolo said trying to play it off. "I'll make an appointment."

It would be his last appointment of the day and his life when Yolo went for her final fitting. He took pride in his work and the finished product was as deadly as the customer wanted them to be.

"What in the world do you plan to do with those young lady?" he had to ask as she practiced chomps in the mirror.

"Kill people," Yolo replied honestly still looking at herself.

"That's nice," he said assuming she was playing. She wasn't. The second he turned his back Yolo pounced. The man yelped in pain when she jumped onto his back and bit into his neck.

A satisfying hot gush of blood filled Yolo's mouth when she bit into his jugular vein. She clamped down and hung on as he thrashed wildly to survive. He would not survive. She went down with him when he dropped to his knees. When he fell face, first she went with him. She stayed on him until she felt the blood stop pumping into her mouth.

"Grrr!" Yolo growled at her reflection with blood dripping from her fangs. It was all too funny to her and she cracked up giggling. "Thanks doc, they're great!"

****

Yolo spent the night before her plane ride researching plane crashes. Although relatively few and far between, the death toll was remarkable. She entertained the thought of shooting a plane down to meet her quota but shook it off. Killa never shot a plane down so she wouldn't either.

"Wish you were on the plane with me," Yolo told the picture of Killa she carried. "I'd take you in the bathroom and fuck you silly."

Yolo stared at that picture while she massaged her throbbing vagina. She called his name when she was about to cum, then blamed it on him when she did.

"Mmm, see what you did?" she asked showing the picture the puddle she produced. The good nut put her down for a good sleep. She needed some rest because she had some killing to do.

The Baron drove Yolo to the airport the next morning. She chatted incessantly to the back of his head from the backseat and he ignored every word of it. Increased security procedures meant she had to arrive hours before her flight's departure. As fate would have it, she ended up in line behind a Muslim man.

Yolo looked the man up and down twisted her lips up at his high water pants and crispy white thobe. He had a big fluffy beard and a dark prostration mark on his handsome caramel face. He felt her staring and turned to face her.

Yolo

"Good morning young lady" he offered with a sweet smile.

"Just don't blow the plane up" Yolo quipped through her own sweet smile.

"Fuck you too young lady," he shot back just as sweetly. Before Yolo got to say something else smart, a T.S.A agent arrived on scene.

"Sa'id Salaam, would you mind stepping out of line for additional screening? We randomly select travelers for extra security," he said courteously.

"Sure," he said and followed him to the room of randomly selected travelers. All Muslim, go figure.

Yolo breezed through security with no problem. She didn't have any weapons since they were waiting in Atlanta. Besides, she was a weapon. Looking like a cute college kid ushered her through security.

"You must be Yolo!" Allo asked when she arrived at the terminal in Atlanta. He had compared the incoming faces against the picture he had.

"And you must be Allo," she shot back and shoved her carryon at him. She recognized him from his picture too. Yup, his ass was in trouble too. The smart mouth little man violated one of the 48 laws of power. He'd offended the wrong person and was going to die for it. He had instructions to pick her up and she had instructions to drop him off.

Rapper Nano got his name from how much he weighed. The five feet four inch man was already small but because he ate more drugs than food, he was grossly underweight. He tipped the scales in a light in the ass 125 pounds.

Nano was a rap star but lived like a rock star. He consumed cocaine, weed, X, pills, alcohol, syrup, pretty much any of everything. He kept a ten-man entourage consisting of a bodyguard, a hype man, a butler, and seven male groupies better known as homeboys. Yolo was delighted to be able to add them to her numbers as well.

The Black Mob had excellent surveillance. They were everywhere and nowhere at the same time all of the time. As a result, Nano popped up everywhere Allo said he would.

"See?" Allo said when the Bentley pulled to a midtown condo where Nano copped the mollies that he popped. "He's going to Lenox next."

"Not bad," Yolo admitted. She couldn't help but snicker at the sight of the rapper up close.

He was a tiny little fellow with a big dreadlocked head. Every visible surface of skin was covered in tattoos. His bright orange skinny jeans hugged his narrow ass and squeezed his balls tightly. Electric blue Chucks and matching derby made him look more like a clown than a rapper. Then again, those lines have been blurred since the nineties.

Big Kodac provided the large security guard for the man knowing he was less than a man. He further protected his investment by putting a life insurance policy on him. It was to offset the inevitable drug overdose in his future. Or unexpected Yolo.

The next stop was upscale Lenox mall. There the rapper would pick out a blouse for the evening and promote his upcoming show. It was also the best place to meet groupies. There's far too much going on to select quality groupies during a show. No, better to pick them up in the daylight and bring them along. Let them hang out backstage since backstage always leads to back shots.

Knowing the emaciated rapper ate the mall pizza when he did eat that's where Yolo waited for him. He arrived in line and scanned her from the bottom up. Nice small feet, firm calves and a round ass under a super short skirt. Once he had seen enough and tapped her on the shoulder.

"Sup shorty?" he asked with his signature platinum grimace.

"Sup with you?" Yolo asked displaying her own fangs.

"Dang dem shits is dope!" Nano cheered and moved in for a closer look.

"Careful, they sharp," she warned and took a playful chomp at him. It was then she realized she wouldn't even need a gun for him. No, she would save the bullets for his team.

"Who did dem? I got to gets me a set!" Nano proclaimed.

"Doctor Kilroy in New York. He…"

"I heard he got kilt!" he gossiped.

"Really?" Yolo asked as if she hadn't murdered the man herself. Grrr… "Guess I got the only set," she shrugged.

"Speaking of sets…you wanna be my guest at my show tonight?" he asked then bust a rapper type pose.

"Show? What are you a magician?" she asked. Just then, she noticed he was wearing a girl's shirt. Was sure too since she had the same shirt, in the same size.

"Nah I ain't no magician. I'm Nano... The rapper Nano?" he asked when she still didn't acknowledge him. "I sing that song 'That's my Bitch' and 'Bitch Please', Bitches be Like', 'Bitch Who',' Who Dat Bitch' and 'B...'"

"You must not like girls very much." Yolo wondered what kind of man would advocate and promote use of the derogatory word so much. Perhaps his mother was a bitch or his daughter. Maybe his wife and sisters were bitches? No shade but if the shoe fits buy a purse to match cuz you're probably a bitch too.

"What? I love bitches!" he insisted. "Come to my show."

"Only if we can hang out after the show," she said tracing her fangs with her tongue seductively.

"Fuck yeah!" Nano cheered showing he did indeed have a little bitch in him too. Yolo scrunched her pretty face and tilted her head at the curious display.

"Are they coming too?" she asked of his crew all staring down her throat. She didn't mind since the 40 caliber held ten shots.

"Shawty my house so big you won't even know they there," he said half truthfully. The house he lived in was indeed big enough to be alone in, even if twenty people were there; it just wasn't his. The house, the cars, and even the jewelry he wore where all assets of the record company.

****

100

"Who is dat bitch over dere? Dats my bitch! What about dat bitch in da chair? That's my bitch! I ain't never gon' switch cuz dats my bitch!" Nano rapped as bitches in the audience rapped along. Even the bitches backstage called themselves bitches along with him.

"I'ma be his bitch tonight," a pretty young groupie dared. She had read so many bitch books and heard so many bitch songs coming from black men she just accepted being a bitch. We could pause for a moment of silence for black pride...

Yolo counted the nine groupies and added them to her tally, which would make 20 plus Allo. Being a girl short meant one of them would have to pull a double. No, not working two shifts but fucking two men. Another moment of silence could go here.

Inside the limo, Nano popped an upper, a downer, licked a line of Mollie, slugged a shot of liquor, fired up a blunt, and sipped on his syrup. He nodded off several times during the ride out to his suburban digs. Yolo was tempted to pluck the blunt from his tattooed fingers but she didn't like the way it sparked and sizzled when he pulled it.

When the convoy of cars arrived, the entourage and groupies all filed in behind Nano. They quickly spread out for places to get their freak on. Yolo followed the woozy rapper.

"In here," Nano directed when they reached the third floor master suite. He groped Yolo's ass when she walked in. She fought the urge to pop him in the mouth. In the end, she let the free feel go, why not since she was about murder him. Or so she thought.

Nano swooned and swayed as he stripped out of his clothes. Yolo stripped too since she didn't bring a change of clothes and planned to get bloody. The only thing in her purse was a plastic pistol and pair of pliers. She giggled at the sight of the naked rapper. He had smoked, snorted, and sipped himself into a tattoo-covered skeleton. Even his dick was shriveled up from abuse and barely visible under the dense bush of pubic hair.

Then, the strangest thing happened. Nano's eye fluttered as he swayed then fell flat on his face. Yolo cocked her head curiously and leaned in to investigate. Nano took a deep breath and exhaled raggedly. He took another but didn't blow that one out. He would take that one to hell with him. The combination of drugs had euthanized him like a puppy. Nano had a strong chemical odor coming out of his pores from the fatal combination of drugs. In fact, he had the perfect mix of drugs in his system to kill certain cancers.

"So! I'm still getting them teeth," Yolo pouted to the corpse. She was in her feelings about not getting to kill the man. Sure, she would get credit for the kill but couldn't count it towards her goal.

Yolo retrieved her pliers and opened the man's mouth. She braced her foot against his face and pulled out the jewels one by one. Luckily poor dental hygiene had them loose making her job a little easier. Once the deed was done, she set out to kill 19 people with ten shots.

Yolo

"Bad girls move in silence and violence," Yolo whispered as she screwed the silencer on the tip of the pistol. Still completely naked, she tipped out into the hallway.

Yolo tilted her head listening for sounds of life so she could go kill. Slurps and moans alerted her to sexual activity in a nearby room. She crept down the hall and peeked in a cracked door. There she was, the head groupie giving the head of security some head. She watched for pointers before pointing the pistol. A round each cancelled the blowjob and Yolo went off in search of more prey. Two down seventeen to go with only eight shots left. She was going to have to get creative.

The barber and hype man were so busy ramming themselves into opposite sides of the groupie pulling double duty that they didn't hear death creep into the room. Killing two birds with one stone is a lot easier then killing two men with one shot especially since they were both moving which made the shot that much more difficult. Yolo was patient though, she waited, waited, waited, and then 'PST.'

"Ten!" she cheered quietly scoring her shot. The bullet passed through the back of the man delivering back shots and entered the forehead of the man getting head. Another trick shot. The groupie looked up just in time to see the flash that made her a memory.

Another trick shot down through the back of a humper and into the humpee left 14 but only four bullets. Those rounds were quickly used on the next two couples. A lovely set of knives in the kitchen got put to new use as she cut, slashed, and stabbed the remaining victim.

Yolo was covered in blood from the different donors once she finished. She placed a call to Allo to come pick her up before jumping into the marble shower. All the excitement had her excited; luckily, the shower had a hand held sprayer. She stepped out clean and relaxed from busting a nut just as Allo texted from the driveway.

"Come in," she texted back and shimmed into her panties and bra.

"Dang! They all dead?" Allo asked as he stepped inside of the massacre scene.

"One left," she said leading him inside. He was too focused on the butt cheeks protruding from the panties to think.

Yolo led him into an unused room and turned to face him. He was her height so they were face to face. Allo tried his luck and leaned in for a kiss. Yolo giggled coyly before running her tongue around his lips. She then sucked his bottom lip into her mouth and bit it clean off.

"The fuck?" he asked in confusion and pain watching her chew on his lip. He reached for it and got popped in his eye. He frowned as if he didn't understand so she popped him in his other eye. Once he understood what was happening he put his scrawny arms up to fight and got beat to death.

Yolo hit him so many times he gave up and tried to run. A quick swipe of her feet tripped him onto his face. She knelt over him and delivered an elbow to the base of his skull that separated his brain from his spine and soul from his body. 82 minus Nano meant 81, 19 to go.

Chapter 14

By 20 Yolo was up to 90 and things grinded to a halt. The previous murders were so brutal that it forced honor amongst thieves. No one wanted to get chopped up so they stepped up and did good business.

The inactivity was driving the killer crazy. She went months without a hit and she was itching to murder something. Luckily for her Playa-D started fucking up and decided to donate to her cause.

"Hey! Make it rain!" Daryl Jones aka Playa-D cheered as he made it rain. He carelessly tossed bills on the stage in at his favorite strip joint.

His favorite stripper, a platinum blonde dubbed Platinum popped, shimmed, and shook under a flurry of bills. They say it ain't tricking if you got it and I say they a damn lie. Especially when it's not your money.

The girl was smart enough to know her pussy was worth more by showing it to the man than giving it to him. She had been a hoe long enough to know that vagina loses its value once a man busts a nut. This of course does not apply to wives.

"Please stop," T-Rock pleaded once more. He was the second in command in the Black Mob Orlando chapter. They had the city and surrounding counties on smash handling all drug sales. It was going so well until Playa-D started fucking up.

T-Rock did all he could do to cover up the fuck up. The payments to Casper got shorter and shorter. Soon he had to come clean to save himself. His friend was a dumb ass and he wasn't going down with him.

Playa-D was a big trick. Besides his wife, he had ten baby mamas. Ten but only seven kids. Several sidepieces plus the strippers and jump offs. Even his mother had her palm out every time he saw her. All that pussy cost. It cost money at first but when they were summoned for a meeting, it was going to cost a lot more. A whole lot more.

"Please stop my ass!" Playa-D shouted as he tossed more money on the stage. "I'm tryna fuck that bitch!"

"That bitch isn't tryna fuck you! Besides, we got a flight to catch in the morning to go meet with Baron," T-Rock reminded.

"The Baron ain't gon' say shit to me," Playa-D laughed. He knew from previous meetings that the man never spoke.

The pasty white man named Casper did all the talking because he actually ran the mob. An older white man used to do all the killing but he disappeared years ago. That's when money started coming short. Casper let him put himself in the air, now it was time to kick away the chair. (Jay-Z)

"Yeah, you right," T-Rock shrugged. He left him tossing his life at the stripper's feet and went to tell his wife about his upcoming promotion.

The next morning T-Rock had to track Playa-D down for the flight. Platinum had chumped him off so he ended up at a baby mama's house. Dude was so busy flirting with the ticket clerk he didn't notice that T-Rock purchased a round trip ticket for himself but one-way for him. He would not be coming back.

Yolo had recently underwent the big chop and cut off her thick crop. Actually, she had a hairdresser cut it then killed her for it. It was a flimsy excuse but she did make number 91. Nine to go.

The short curly cut looked great on her cute face but also served practical purposes. It allowed her to rock an array of wigs that concealed and changed her identity. By far her favorite wig was the blond dreadlocks. It was heavy because the thick dreads as well as cap were made from bullet proof Kevlar.

She pulled on the wig and stepped into a tiny skirt over the leopard panties. A tight half t-shirt and sandals later she slinked into the boardroom where the meeting had begun.

Casper had already slapped Big Rock for declining sales in Baltimore. He blamed it on some outsiders from New York who came down and set up shop. Yolo drew slight attention as she swung her curvy little hips in the room. Most men shot a quick glace and turned back to the speaker. Not Playa-D though. He locked on the girl licking his lips lustfully watching her every step.

T-Rock tried to kick him under the table to alert him to the fact that Casper was calling his name. When Yolo plopped wide legged into a chair he zeroed in on the leopard print covered rabbit. The rest of the men could only shake their heads at what was to come. They gave him one last look knowing he would never be seen again. Not unless you wanted to go sifting through pig shit for him and ain't nobody got time for that.

"Mr. Daryl I have called your name five times but you're more concerned with the goings on between Yolo's legs than in your own city," Casper explained after slapping him viscously across his check.

"No," he replied like a child as he raised his hand to the welts rising from the slap. He didn't even hear the question he said 'no' to.

"You think if Yolo were to take you in the other room and suck your dick it would help your concentration?" he asked like a gracious host. What a great host!

A few of the men in attendance closed their eyes tightly and tried to beam him telepathic signals to shut the fuck up. Others shook their heads tersely hoping he would shut the fuck up. Only he would not shut the fuck up. Dumb ass nodded his head in agreement with what on the surface sounded like a good idea.

"You know what? A nigga is a lil uptight. Long ass plane ride. A good blowjob might take the edge off," he agreed, with his dumb ass.

Yolo

Yolo couldn't help laughing at the statement. She was going to take the edge off alright. She stood up and extended her small hand to lead the man off to slaughter. The second they cleared the room T-Rock was congratulated on his promotion.

"In here," Yolo directed stepping aside so her victim could enter. He stepped in, in one piece, but would not leave the same way.

"Yolo that short for Yolonder? I got a cousin named Yolonder," he said making small talk.

"Nah, it's an acronym," she replied alluding to you only live once. Of course, she had no way of knowing how or why she was named, but guessed correctly. You only live once.

"If you suck this real good I'ma let you ride it," Playa-D announced as he produced his semi erect dick and stroked it.

"That'll be a first," she chuckled at the generous offer.

Yolo had been too busy killing to think about boys. Not to mention Killa had her heart so she was saving her cherry for him. Since she was fond of the outfit and didn't want to ruin it she stepped out of it and put it in a drawer.

When she knelt in front of him he handed his now rock hard cock to her and leaned back royally. She took it with one hand and reached under the bed with the other. That's where She-Ra's bag was. Yup, same bag with the knives.

"Ouch! Damn!" Daryl griped when Yolo bit the head sharply.

"So sorry," Yolo giggled and bowed like a geisha girl. She planted loud kisses were she bit to ease the pain. It did the

111

trick and he laid back down. Yolo took him in her mouth slowly and gently and then bit him again. This time she bit him harder at the base of the shaft causing him to pop up again. When he did, she locked eyes and slid him back into her mouth.

The player watched her work her head and hands until he was satisfied she would not bite him again. She didn't, the next time he laid back she pulled out the knife. The super sharp blade cut through the hard dick like a hot knife through soft butter. Playa-D winced from the dull pain and looked up to see Yolo still sucking his dick. A second later, he realized she was standing up. He looked down to where his dick should have been just in time to see a long arch of blood skeet with his heartbeat.

"Give me that!" he insisted planning to put it back. Sure, it wasn't a rational request, but in his defense, he just got his dick cut off. Give him a break.

"I used to be scared of dick. Now I throw lips to the shit" Yolo ripped into the severed penis as she scampered away.

Of course, Playa-D gave chase; she did have his dick after all. He chased her around the small room losing more blood with every step. He almost had her when he grabbed a handful of dreads. Yolo shook her head and came out of the wig and got away.

Playa-D ran out of steam and dropped to his knees. He reached out for his dick and fell onto his face. He looked so sad when he passed Yolo felt sorry for him.

"Here then," she offered apologetically and put his penis in his pocket.

Yolo showered, changed, and arrived back in the boardroom just as Casper announced the solution to the problem Big Rock was having in his city. Her.

"Yolo pack a bag. You're going to Baltimore."

"Body more, Murda-land!" she cheered at the violent nickname for the violent city. She was ready and willing to go killing but an unexpected problem in Atlanta popped up first.

Chapter 15

"Boss we got a problem in Atlanta!" Nut said via intercom. As he spoke he spoke he cued up footage from security cameras. Casper recognized the upscale Atlanta home and shook his head.

"Dallas no doubt," Casper grumbled. The man had recently earned a spot on the shit/hit list for skimming money.

"Is this live?"

"No. It's from a couple of hours ago," Nut replied as the footage showed a cable guy knocking on the door. The angle changed and Yolo got a good look at a face she knew very well.

"Killa!" she cheered feeling moisture flood her boy shorts.

"I've heard of this guy. We could use a guy like this on our team," Casper said watching him easily gain entry to the secure home.

"Don't seem like much of a killer to me?" Nut wondered as the lady of the home verbally abused him while he pretended to fix the cable he disabled. Yolo was about to recite his deadly stats but Dallas pulled up and the show began.

"Hey baby, who dat?" the handsome heavily jeweled man asked grabbing a kiss along with a handful of ass.

"Hey, hun, the cable out, and they sent this idiot to..." was all she got out before the gun came out.

"You! Hands in the air. And you shut the fuck up!" Killa grunted from behind a large pistol. Yolo came instantly.

"Really?" Casper asked when he saw her dilemma. He shook his head and turned back to the violent robbery on the screen.

In Dallas's defense, he didn't give up easily. Why would he let someone steal what he had stolen? Even when Killa threatened to kill him, his woman, the baby, plants, and fish he remained tight-lipped. It wasn't until he raised an ax over the sleeping child that the woman blurted out the combination to the safe.

"You nosey bitch! How you get my codes?" Dallas demanded lying face down with his hand tied behind his back.

"Bitch? You would let him kill our baby to keep your precious money!" Candy shouted.

"Ain't my kid," he shrugged. He knew the intruder still needed to get past the fingerprint and retina scan before he could get into the safe. Killa knew it too, that's what the ax was for. "And it's still one more number."

"Ok," Killa laughed. "I will chop your hand off and pop out your eye. Either way you coming off that cash"

"Kill him and I'll give you the number," his lady pleaded. They had just broken up.

"Ok," Killa shrugged and raised the gun to shoot.

"Wait! I want this to be the last thing he sees," Candy said kneeling in front of Killa. She glanced over to ensure her child was asleep and grudge sucked the robber. Once she swallowed, she had one more request, well two.

"Let me kill him," she pleaded reaching for the gun. Killa shrugged and handed it to her making sure to stay close enough to prevent her from turning on him.

It was an unnecessary precaution because she squeezed off three silent shots the second she got the gun. Killa kept his word about popping out the eyes and cutting off the hand. The body allowed him partial access to the safe. Candy used the remaining number to bargain 25% of the take.

"So where the fuck is my money!" Casper shouted like a spoiled brat.

"We tracked the thief via satellite pictures and a tracking device in the bag. We also intercepted a satellite call he made," Nut proudly reported. "The woman checked into a hotel with the kid."

"Go kill them both," Casper demanded causing Yolo to gasp.

"Both?" she screeched in fear of losing her idol.

"Yeah the girl and the kid. I have plans for this Killa. He's about to work for me!"

****

Killa smiled brightly at the duffle bag full of cash. That smile beamed brighter when his satellite phone began to ring. Knowing it could only be one person, he eagerly took the call.

"Hey Grandma, everything ok?"

"No everything is not ok," Casper said in that sarcastic tone that was going to get him killed one day.

"A-yo, I don't know how you got that phone," Killa growled sounding more animal than human. "If anything has happened to my people I'm going to murder everyone you've ever met in your life. Your family, friends, classmates from third grade, your mailman, the ..."

"Oh stop being so dramatic, your family is fine; we're only barbarians when we need to be. Your chief concern right now should be the return of that duffle bag full of BM money."

"Who are you?" Killa asked looking at the bag and wondering how the caller knew how to reach him. He knew all too well that some people are not to be fucked with. He was one of them and it appeared he robbed one. Still he couldn't help to ask... "BM? Baby mama? She gave me some head and I may fuck her later."

"She is already dead so you may not wanna fuck her. Unless you like that sort of thing? Oh and B.M is Black Mob. Answer the door and return the money," Casper replied smugly.

"The do..." Killa began to ask but was interrupted by a knock. Killa knew then that he had indeed fucked with the wrong people. He opened the door gun high and was met with one aiming back at him.

"You don't want to do that," an Atlanta police officer warned. "The bag."

Killa was dumbfounded as he handed the duffle bag filled with cash to the cop. In return, the cop handed him a cell phone and backed out of the door. The fancy phone rang immediately.

"Hello?" he asked even though he knew who it was, who else could it be?

"Very good. Now go spend time with that pretty Kitty of yours. We'll be in touch soon," Casper said and hung up.

Being a hired gun did not sit well with Killa but he knew he didn't have much of a choice. The Black Mob knew everything about him but he knew nothing of them. All he could come up with was farfetched tales about a little white man with a mean murder game. He would go along and play ball getting paid for what he did so well. First chance he got he would find and kill them all.

Until then he would enjoy some of the perks the organization offered. The state of the art phone was cool but even cooler when he disabled the GPS. Then had the signal routed all over the globe before reaching him making the phone un-traceable.

Next was the luxury sedan with all the bells and whistles. Among the amenities, Killa found at least four tracking devices. He left them in place allowing them to trace him to the downtown Atlanta condo.

"Nice!"

Kitty purred like Kitty purrs when kitty likes something. "It is" Kitty nodded in agreement when they stepped into the plush unit.

As he scanned the front room, he correctly placed out 8 of the 10 cameras. He stared into one making eye-to-eye contact with Yolo making her giggle like a girl.

"Strip," Killa ordered as he unbuckled his belt. Someone wanted a show so he decided to give them one. "Let's christen the place."

"You so nasty," Kitty giggled and complied. She reached behind her back to unzip her dress. The cute dress fell to the plush carpet revealing all of that good size 16 loving that Killa loved so much.

"Yeah and you love my nasty. What's on the menu?"

The couple had become sexually synced and knew just how to please each other. They even came up with names for the variety of sexual positions they employed.

"Let's start with a vagina appetizer followed by the sidewinder and finish up with back shots," Kitty suggested now that they were naked.

"Coming right up," he eagerly agreed. Even though she didn't offer any head she still knelt in front of him to give him some.

"Pst!" Yolo sucked her teeth loudly as Kitty inched him down he throat. She crossed her arms angrily and turned sideways, but still watched the surveillance monitor.

"Told you I would do it," Yolo pouted as Killa worked his lips, tongue, and hand in a magical medley. When Killa took position between the big caramel thighs, she really pouted. "Ugh!"

Yolo watched in lustful amazement as Killa lapped at Kitty's kitty. Her hand found its way into the puddle in her panties and that's how Casper found her when he walked in.

"Get a room," he laughed. "Good news, you'll be meeting him soon. You're going back to Atlanta."

The thought of meeting her crush sent her over the edge. As soon as Casper cleared the room, she came hard with a loud grunt. She walked out on Killa delivering firm back shots that echoed in the quiet condo.

Yolo boarded a plane to Atlanta later that evening. She printed a picture of Killa to keep her company for the flight. As soon as they were airborne, she pulled it out for a chat.

"So...you liked when that girl went down on you?" she asked feeling a little jealous. "Yeah I guess you do, guys like head. I won't mind doing it for you, you know. I..."

"Aww how sweet. Is that your boyfriend?" the lady seated next to her asked seeing her talking to the picture. "A cutie."

"Yes, we..." Yolo turned and smiled until she realized that the lady was a man. "So, you think my man is cute?" she asked with a smile that hid her murderous intention. If he said yes, she was going to kill him.

"Girl yes!" the homosexual gushed snatching the picture to gawk closely at him.

"Let's grab a bite to eat when we get to Atlanta," Yolo suggested sweetly. He agreed and made a date with his own murder. He made number 93. She was almost there.

Yolo met her crush the next day with mixed emotions. She was helplessly in love but none too pleased that he got the nod to do double murder instead of her. She did have a quota to meet after all. Instead of taking the lead, she was tasked to baby-sit the victims until Killa arrived to kill them.

The crooked D.A and piece of shit public defender really needed killing. They had tag teamed plenty of un-suspecting defenders into prison. Now was payback time. A relative of a man put to death contracted the Black Mob to return the favor.

Posing as a prostitute Yolo got the men to an out of the way hotel. She kept them company until the star of the show crept in the room. She fought the urge to scream 'OMG!' when he walked in gun first.

The tall beige man stole her breath with an audible gasp. The six-foot Killer was pretty in pictures but gorgeous in person. She stared up at him like a girl in love until he yelled at her.

"You! Out!" Killa demanded following orders to let the girl go. If not for strict instructions not to kill her, he would have. He did steal a glance at her curvy little curves as she dressed. Should have got a good look at the face behind the dreads.

"Don't look so tough to me," Yolo huffed in a fit of professional jealousy once she was back outside. With that a rivalry was born. Just like Casper planned.

Chapter 16

"S…so…so…so Casper said just kill the M…Menendez br…br…brothers r…r…right?" Big Rock st, st, st, stuttered as they rode back from the airport with their guest murderer. He wanted to know now so he could catch a flight to anywhere but here.

"Y, ye, ye, yes" Yolo giggled at his cowardice. Here he was this big black man with two bodyguards scared of a girl.

Her orders where simply to murder the brothers from New York who set up shot in B-More. Hence the saying you gotta B-more careful. The city already, had a high murder rate but it was about to get higher.

The Menendez brothers, Gabby and Pedro had a mean murder game. Every time Big Rock sent a hitter to hit them, they sent them back dead. He lost man after man until Casper sent Yolo. Sometimes the best man for the job is a girl.

One of Big Rocks bodyguards called Bull didn't know any better and kept flirting. He had undressed her with his eyes from the second she stepped off the plane. Now in the car he stole a glance at her legs from the back seat.

"They hang out at a strip joint called Head or Tails. Word is they some freaks. Like running trains on young girls," Bull said turning all the way around and trying to peak between her legs.

"Pussy will get you killed every time," Yolo said seductively with a sinister smirk. She parted her legs a little to prove her point. It was bait; all he had to do was bite.

Bull was a smart guy and heard the threat. He turned back in his seat and continued the conversation through the rearview mirror.

"The club manager is another trick named Steve. He personally...screws all the new dancers. The back of their throats that is," Bull laughed.

The limo pulled to a stop in front of one of Baltimore's finest five star hotels. This was where Big Rock put her up to be as far away from his suburban home as possible. Yolo didn't plan to stay long. She intended to murder the men and head back to New York that night.

****

"Here's the new one," Jo-Jo announced after tapping on the office door. The man inside barked his instructions to enter.

Yolo stumbled slightly on her special six-inch stilettos. She had been practicing how to use the deadly shoes until proficient, walking however, was another story. The heels of the shoes were actually stainless steel daggers. A pair of round balls covered the tips when not in use. The only weapons she carried was the super sharp knife she nicknamed the emasculator. That and her killer smile.

"Youse a pretty little bitch ain't you?" Steve asked as a compliment. If he ever stood a chance of surviving the encounter, it just went out the window. Calling Yolo a bitch was a verbal suicide note.

"Thank you," Yolo smiled and ran her tongue over the platinum fangs.

"A'ight, let me see what you working with," the manager demanded leaning back in the plush leather chair.

Yolo misunderstood and began winding her hips to the music leaking into the office from the sound systems. Steve frowned at the movements and clarified himself.

"Whoa, whoa! Fuck shakin' yo' ass. Let me see what that head working with," he ordered and whipped out his dick. When Yolo came around the desk and knelt, he handed it to her. "Here"

Yolo took it in one hand and pulled the knife with the other. When Steve leaned back, she sliced it off and handed it back, "Here."

"What the fu...," he began to gripe, but Yolo cut him off. She shoved one of the spiked heels into his neck and barely got out of the way of the gush of blood.

"Go to the light Carole Aaannn...oops, Steeeve," Yolo sang as he desperately tried to keep his blood in his body where he needed it. It certainly couldn't benefit him from the floor beneath him.

"Did I get the job?" Yolo asked as she danced some more. She shimmed, popped, and dropped until his head dropped onto his chest. Yolo took that as a yes. "Thank you, thank you!"

The man bled out so quickly that he was on the other side before Yolo got to the other side of the door. She locked the door behind her so he would not be disturbed. Dead people don't like that.

Yolo made her way through the club and found the dressing room. She frowned at the strong aroma of so many vagina sharing the same space. It only took a few seconds to figure out who was in charge. A forty something lesbian barked orders like the manager that she was.

"Excuse me. Steve said I could start tonight," Yolo offered meekly as yet another disguise. Roshawn twisted up her lips and looked the girl over. She wasn't thick like the other girls and had a faraway look in her eyes. Same look Killa had, they saw dead people.

"Must got some good ass head," Roshawn said knowingly. "I might have to get a little of it too once you come off stage."

"Why don't I give you the same thing I gave Steve?" Yolo asked eager to please.

"I want exactly what you gave Steve," she replied lustfully. She had no idea of the brutal murder that awaited. At least she couldn't get her dick cut off though and that was a good thing.

"You got outfits? If not you can get one out the bin and pay for it once you come off stage."

"Yes please," Yolo said and followed Roshawn to a locker full of hoe clothes. Luckily, for her, Roshawn picked an outfit out for her.

"Here you can be Betty Rubble," she snickered handing over a Flintstones looking dress. "Them some bad ass shoes girl!"

"Practical too," Yolo agreed. She accepted the dress and found a locker. After changing from her short skirt to an even shorter one Yolo hit the club.

"Uh, oh," she muttered to herself when she saw the girls in action. These thick stallions worked the poles like gymnast. How was she supposed to attract her victims with that type of competition?

"Steve needs to get some new hoes in here," Gabby Mendez griped as he and his brother Pedro stepped inside their hangout. Not that something was wrong with the hoes on hand, it was just that he, and his brother had ran through them all. Several times apiece. New pussy made their world go around and they wanted some new pussy. Who could blame them?

"Fo' real though," Pedro agreed having grown tired of the same old vaginas.

"Wet-Wet center stage. White Chocolate stage left and Yo, Yoyo...Yolo? Yolo stage right," the DJ announced. Yolo giggled when the DJ threw on the late rapper Nano's ode to stripper bitches entitled "Stripper Bitches."

Wet-Wet showed why she was a star immediately when she hit the stage. The veteran pole dancer hit the pole and slid up, upside down. Once she reached the top, she spun slowly around blowing kisses at the audience with her vagina lips.

The crowd went wild just as they should. The brothers Mendez had sexed her so many times, so many ways they didn't even look her way.

The girl called White Chocolate was a white girl known for one-minute blowjobs. If you lasted past 61 seconds in her mouth, you got your money back. She hadn't issued a refund yet. She could hook four guys up during the average commercial break. If worst came to worst she could take the edge off but that's not what they were looking for. Gabby glanced stage right and found it.

"The fuck?" he exclaimed and stood. Yolo was sitting Indian style playing in her pussy causing him to approach as if in a trance.

"Move! Move out the way!" Tank boomed clearing a path for his trick ass employers.

Just as the brothers reached the stage, Yolo scrunched up her face and bust a nut. A gush of P.J (Pussy Juice) soaked her box and dripped onto the stage below her. The brothers had seen enough.

"Go tell Steve we're taking this bitch with us!" Pedro demanded sending the bodyguard in motion.

"You, get dressed!" Gabby said into her vagina as if it was an ear.

Yolo stood and wobbled slightly from the strong nut and six inch heels. She rushed back to the dressing room on spaghetti legs to get dressed. Once they got into the luxury sedan Yolo sat in the middle of the back seat and went for seconds. Pedro swerved from time to time trying to watch the show through the rearview mirror as he drove. His brother turned all the way around and watched as she came again.

Gabby snatched Yolo from the back seat the second his brother pulled into their reserved space. Pedro put his finger into the puddle she left and tasted it, with his nasty ass. Inside, a coin was tossed to see who got which end of the girl first.

"Heads!" Gabby called out hopefully as the quarter tumbled in the air. Him being a head man he wanted inside her mouth.

"Heads it is!" his brother announced when the coin landed. It was cool with him since he was an ass man himself.

Meanwhile Yolo glanced around the condo for weapons to kill them with. Pedro's use of the bitch word made her want to beat him to death.

"Here," Gabby demanded inching his inches towards her face. She popped the protective balls off the shoes and got ready. Pedro lifted her legs in the air to inspect her pretty juice box.

She opened her mouth to allow Gabby inside. The second his dick head entered, she clamped down and thrust the daggers forward. Pedro was blinded for life but fortunately, that wouldn't be very long. He fell back into the glass table splashing the glass like water. He was the lucky one.

"Yeeowe!" Gabby belted as the razor sharp teeth cut into his meat. Yolo covered up like a boxer to absorb the heavy blows he threw to dislodge her.

He wailed away with both hands and slung his body attempting to get away. It wasn't until the fangs met that he got free. Minus his dick head and that's not really free now is it?

"Here since you want it so bad," Yolo spat after she spat it back at him. What was she gonna do with it anyway? It bounced off his chest and he went after it. Yolo picked up a heavy glass ashtray and swung it with all of her might.

"Bitch I'ma..."Gabby started to say until the next blow knocked the threat along with several teeth back down his throat.

Yolo beat that man like a Hebrew slave who stole something, and that's pretty bad. When he lifted his arms to block the blows they were both broken. Somewhere along the beating, he accepted defeat and gave up. Death was a part of the life that he had chosen so no sense in bitching up when his turn came. He lowered his head in offering and she took him up on it. With one last swing, she split his wig and ended his life.

"Now for the blind man," Yolo stated as she stepped over the corpse. Pedro was wallowing in the broken glass holding his empty eye sockets. "You don't look so good."

"Gabby! Gabby get this bitch! Kill this bitch!" he screamed sounding just like a bitch. He was going to have to scream a lot louder than that for his brother to hear him. Or wait a second and tell him in person.

"Un uh, the bitch killed Gabby," she sang. "Told you to leave Baltimore. You guys came together so you can leave together."

Yolo

Yolo stomped a deadly heel into his lung. She enjoyed the squeal he let out and did it again. And again and again until she was jumping up and down on the man. Somewhere along the line, he caught up with his brother.

Taking a page from Mr. Grimsly's textbook, she ruptured the gas line and lit a candle. Knowing the brothers wouldn't mind she borrowed their Benz and drove to the airport. 94 down, six to go.

Chapter 17

After Yolo returned from the Baltimore murders things ground to a halt. There were lots of people who needed killing but she couldn't get a green light to go kill them. She made the mistake of telling Casper how close to her goal she was and he used it to control her. He was a controlling piece of shit like that. He could have easily sent her on a quadruple or a couple of double homicides but wouldn't. Instead, he sent his newest hired gun Killa. Casper guessed correctly that it would create animosity between her and him. After all, one can't have two of the nation's most prolific killers in cahoots can one?

All she could do was wait and hope. Wait for someone else to fuck up and hope to get the call to go kill them. To ease the monotony her free time was spent in her two favorite pastimes, murder, and masturbation. She watched the footage of Killa and Kitty in the condo more times than was healthy. She would always join in and make it a long distance threesome. To make matters worse the couple would pop into the condo, copulate for the cameras, and leave. Killa would often stare directly into one of the hidden cameras as he showed out.

"If I ever catch you anywhere, any time I'm going to kill you," Yolo told Kitty on the screen. "Broad daylight, mall, church, anywhere."

In Yolo's twisted little mind her and Killa were a couple. Kitty was stealing her time with her man and had to die.

Her other hobby was watching crime scenes from around the globe. She was fascinated by Al-Qaeda and I.S.I.S until she found out that terrorism is actually forbidden in Islam. Reports of recent beheadings in Central America caught her attention. Someone was killing women and keeping their heads. She paused to reflect on starting her own collection of body parts until multiple murders in the Bronx stole her thoughts away.

'In what police are calling the midnight massacre ten men were found dead in the University Homes projects. There are no witnesses and police have no leads...'

"Oh I know who did this," Yolo sang. It had his name written all over it so she had to go see for herself. She felt a sense of pride as she sped towards the city to investigate.

Killa was already back in Atlanta when the first bodies turned up. Even though he was long gone, Yolo could still feel his presence. The hairs on her arm stood up and moisture seeped into her panties.

"Dang my baby aired this shit out," Yolo marveled as she walked into the deserted courtyard. The entire projects were eerily quiet. There were no birds, no squirrels, even the breezed died out. Perhaps he killed them too.

As she sat on a park bench, the bodies began to come out. Two from one building, three from two more. In all ten bodies where collected from around the housing project. She sat there basking in the murderous wake for hours. Even after life in the P.J's began to move again.

Yolo sat there watching people come and go not realizing that the pretty elderly lady with her pretty granddaughter was Killa's grandma and niece. She casually watched them walk by until a familiar name rang in her ear.

"Xavier if you behave yourself you can get a toy. One toy!" Sincerity stressed as she lead her son through the courtyard.

Knowing that was Killa's born name she instantly slipped into a rage. She knew he had a son named Xavier who lived with his aunt but she would not allow any more children. She would have pulled her gun and gunned that boy and his mother down on the spot had he looked like her man. Seeing the child bore no resemblance to either Killa or his mother she correctly assumed he was fathered by someone else.

"Whew!" Yolo said to herself when she returned from her murderous rage.

Unauthorized killings where more than just frowned upon in the Black Mob. You needed permission to hit someone from Casper himself. In fact, quite a few of Yolo's 96 confirmed kills were violators of that rule. They ran a tight ship; you kill who you're told to kill.

Casper had ears and eyes everywhere so she wasn't surprised when he connected him to the murders. When she arrived back at the Long Island mansion, he was scolding her boo for the freelance work. He was really putting it on too, being quite rude and sarcastic. That's no way to talk to a killer. Definitely no way to talk to Killa.

"What's wrong?" Yolo asked when Casper hung up the phone.

"Your so-called boyfriend. He went on an unauthorized killing spree. Personal not business. I fined him this time but next time he gets a spanking," Casper said as if he was the one who actually did the spanking.

"Want me to go to Atlanta and kill his girlfriend?" she asked ready to catch the next flight out if given a nod.

"Nah, not yet, Wait until the next time he fucks up. And trust me, he'll fuck up again," Casper replied admitting that he couldn't control the man.

"Oh, ok," Yolo pouted like the spoiled brat that she was.

"Oh cut it out," he chuckled. "Don't worry I got someone else who may need killing. An accountant who can't count. If he gives you what he took let him live."

"If not?" she asked eagerly.

"If not then you get to try out the D.C. 2000!"

****

"Please, please, please be home," Yolo pleaded as she drove to the home of Thaddeus and Philomena Frank. Together they would make number 97 and 98. No way was she trying to find that money.

Not to mention she was eager to try out the Decapitator 2000 that just arrived. She went so crazy about the device she saw in a movie that she begged Casper to get her one made.

Yolo

She had instructions to take a hand for the theft if he returned the money. If not, off with his head.

Yolo pulled into the circular driveway of the Frank home and parked. She adjusted the tiny Girl Scout looking outfit and got out. Instead of cookies, she carried a bag full of torture and killing tools. Behind her back was a powerful air gun that could kill without making a sound.

"You rang!" Yolo bellowed like Lurch when she used the huge ornate doorknockers. They were only for show but set off chimes throughout the fancy house.

"Well hello," an elderly butler said politely upon answering the door. "And how can I help you?"

"Oh! Oh! You're 99! You're 99!" Yolo cheered bouncing up and down as she added him to her twisted tally.

"Oh no dear…I'll only be 70 next week," the gentleman chuckled.

"Nuh uh," Yolo sang and shot him in his smile. The burst of air shattered his dentures sending fragments into his brain.

Yolo stepped over the dead man like he was a puddle and closed the door behind her. She nodded approvingly at the grand foyer of imported marble. She did a little tap dance and giggled at the sound echoing in the large space. Hearing sounds of life she inched forward to kill.

"Hello?" Yolo asked Mrs. Frank when she found her nursing her baby in the nursery.

"Oh! You startled me! Where is Mr. Stewart?" Philomina asked.

"I don't really know," she admitted with a curious frown. She often wondered herself where people went after she killed them. She didn't yet know that they entered the state of the grave to await judgment day. Judgment day was definitely coming.

"Where's your husband?" Yolo said moving to something easier.

"Your guess is as good as mine," Mrs. Frank huffed. She long ago gave up on trying to keep tabs on the man. She had enough dildos to fuck herself properly so fuck him. Just then, Thaddeus came in on his way out.

"Honey I have a thing at the club eh...oh my!" Mr. Frank said before a look at sexy black girl caught the lie in his throat. "And who might you be young lady?"

"I might be a Girl Scout who came to suck your dick in front of your wife...but I'm not. Casper sent me to collect the money you stole."

"I...um I don't...what money?" Thaddeus asked to Yolo's delight. Out came the gun and they marched to the dining room.

Mrs. Frank only reluctantly handed her baby over when Yolo demonstrated the air gun. When it shattered a ten thousand dollar vase, she did as she was told. Yolo held the baby as the wife secured the husband. Next, Mrs. Frank was plastic cuffed to a chair.

"Cute baby," Yolo offered once she finally took a look at the child.

"Yes, she's an angel," Mrs. Frank pleaded desperately.

"She's about to be," Yolo replied ready to give her wings. "Hey! Are babies real people? I mean do they count as whole people?"

"Of course! They are real, whole people just as important as adults!" Philomena stressed. She relaxed a little from the look of elation the answer gave the intruder. It was of course the wrong answer and got the child added to the tally.

"Great!" she cheered and skipped happily into the kitchen with the child. The child saw the smile and smiled back. She cooed and kicked her little feet until Yolo tossed her into the sink full of sudsy dishwater. The baby added a few more bubbles as it struggled to live, and then died.

"Just like a chicken," she recalled as she diced the child up according to a recipe for lamb kabobs.

Yolo ignored the couples pleas, questions, and demands as she breezed back through the dining room. She hopped up the steps and pretended to look for money. Since finding the money was the last thing on her demented mind she went through all their shit. Her nosey little ass avoided anywhere the money could be in favor of being nosey.

"Cute," she said to a sexy maid uniform she stumbled across in the 'hers' closet. She quickly stripped and changed into it. She also discovered that Mr. wasn't laying much pipe. At home anyway, because Mrs. had a large assortment of do it yourself dicks. Thaddeus would often tell her to go fuck herself not knowing she did just that.

Once enough time had elapsed, she went back down stairs and served dinner. You know from the prologue how that turned out. Kill number 99 and 100 with two weeks to spare.

Chapter 18

Yolo could only bask in her glory for a short time. News of a lodge bombing that claimed over a hundred lives had Killa written all over it. Casper decided to send another message as well as drive a wedge between Yolo and her crush. They could never be allowed to become friends. Can you imagine Killa and Yolo on the same team?

"So…I hear your boyfriend just had a baby?" he asked as if he did not know.

"A wha…?" Yolo gasped as the heart breaking news knocked the air from her lungs. She had come to grips with the fact that he had a child with relatives in Philly but another one…

"Yeah, seems like he had another girlfriend besides you. Don't worry; mom and child are doing fine at Lincoln Hospital in the Bron…" Casper said and laughed when she bolted from the room.

Yolo made it all the way to her truck before realizing she wasn't dressed. She rushed back inside and donned one of her many disguises. A pair of colorful scrubs and matching sneakers was perfect for the occasion. She pulled a short red wig on and was back down the steps.

She arrived in the Bronx in record time and rushed up to the maternity ward. Yolo's heart broke so hard it could be felt and heard. To make matters worse, this was the same chick she had seen in the projects after the midnight massacre.

"I should have killed her and her big head son," she mumbled to herself. The newborn was a spitting image of his dangerous dad. He had his chin, his nose, and eyes. Those piercing brown eyes.

She breezed around the room for hours until he came. In walked the beautiful man in the flesh. He had the smooth gait of a king yet humble as a peasant. He was Killa.

"Oh my god, oh my god," Yolo chanted, fanning herself when she saw the rock star. She decided she had to go in and get a closer look. Had to, besides her panties couldn't get any wetter.

"Is everything ok?" she sang as she breezed into the room. She and Killa locked eyes for a second that seemed like a month. He frowned one of those 'where do I know you from' frowns at the faint recognition. She picked up the chart and nodded as she read it like she understood it. When she saw the patient's name and address, she decided to keep it. She smiled and walked out just as grandma walked in.

Yolo drove home with tears in her eyes. She wanted to be the one laying in a hospital bed with her hair all over the place and dry crusty lips. She pleaded with Casper to let her kill the mother and child but was denied. Instead, he sent her back a week later to take pictures of her with his child to use as a threat.

The threat was taken seriously and the veteran killer sent his family into hiding. As bad as Yolo wanted to kill them she had missed her chance. Luckily, for her, Casper had someone who really needed killing. Big Kodac was back in town.

****

Big Kodac had been in hiding for over a year. He figured time had passed and the heat would be off. Boy was he wrong. The big man had made a fortune from the death of his star rapper. Not only did the insurance company pay off but also his sales went through the roof. They even released a new cd of unreleased songs entitled 'Bitches Gon' Miss Me When I'm Gone.' He was right too, bitches did miss him, and the album went double platinum.

New money meant new digs for the Kodac family. They traded their Atlanta mansion for an even bigger one. Of course, Yolo did her homework and figured her way in. The only security was a large bodyguard and three large presa de carnario dogs roaming the yard. The dogs were big and vicious but young, still puppies. Yolo made sure to visit with them each night with a treat. She covered chicken parts with human blood and they loved it. When the time was ripe, she made her move.

"Yeah!" the large guard yelled at Yolo when he answered the intercom.

"I'm the new cook," she said sweetly, looking into the camera. No one could dispute that she was the new cook since she had killed the old one.

"Can you fry chicken!" he demanded as if he'd turn her away if she couldn't.

"Of course!" she lied. She could boil a baby but other than that, Yolo wasn't much use in the kitchen.

"Ok then! Hold up, I gotta walk you in cuz the dogs might eat you," he said and came out. To his surprise, the dogs were at the gate wagging their tails happily at the friend.

"Is this the nanny?" Mrs. Kodac asked thrusting her child at her before she could answer. "My husband and I are going out, take care of the kids, cook dinner, and feed them damn dogs!"

"Ok," Yolo giggled since she planned to do all of that anyway. Just not in that order. Big Kodac scowled at Yolo as he passed through on his way out. He ran his eyes up and down her petite frame and cracked a smile. A last minute wink said that he couldn't wait to get her alone. Yolo winked back because the feeling was mutual.

"Ouch!" Yolo whelp when an object hit her leg. She frowned down at the toy truck and then the rambunctious little boy who threw it.

"You gotta come play with me!" the brat demanded.

"Ok," she sang along with a fake smile. She followed him into the playroom and strangled him. "Fun ain't it?"

The bodyguard was next to go. She fixed him a ham, cheese, and cyanide sandwich and watched as he died. Now it was time to cook dinner.

Ask any cannibal and they'll tell you the best meat of a baby comes from the thigh. Accordingly, that's where the lunatic began. It would have been nice if Yolo had killed the child first before extracting that good thigh meat but she isn't

Yolo

exactly nice now is she? While she may not be very nice, she isn't wasteful either. She opened the back door and tossed the screaming child to the dogs. It was just an appetizer; the main course was yet to come.

****

"Dinner is served," Yolo sang proudly when the Kodac couple returned. Again, he devoured her with his eyes while she turned her lips up.

"Where are the kids?" Mrs. Kodac asked wondering why her annoying son hadn't swooped in to annoy her the second she walked in.

"Um...gone? With um...Ray," she replied.

"Where they go?" Mr. Kodac asked curiously. Not that he cared, he was just asking.

"I'm not really sure," Yolo replied wondering again, where dead people went once they died. "Welp let's eat."

This was another one of those 'bad to worse' scenarios. Feeding a child to its parents is bad but adding poison is worse. Mrs. Kodac falling face first into her baby on her plate was bad but Mr. Kodac continuing to eat was worse. He fell out of his chair once he finished eating his baby. Mrs. Kodac dying from the poison was bad but Mr. Kodac waking up hours later was worse, far...far worse.

"What? Where? When?" Big Kodac stammered as he blinked awake. He looked around trying to figure out his predicament and saw Yolo.

"You forgot how," she teased. The taunt was bad but the explanation was worse.

145

"Where, is your basement. What is you're dead, and when is now. Oh and here comes the how," Yolo said opening the door letting the dogs in.

"Casper? I'll pay you whatever he paid you to spare me! I'll double it if you go kill him!" Kodac pleaded as he strained against his restraints. He was bleeding profusely from the slashes Yolo cut into his legs, arms, and torso.

"In the words of your late buddy Nano, bitch nah!" she giggled and released the hounds. "Can't be called man eaters until you eat a man."

The dogs didn't catch the statement but did like the blood. They ran over to the naked man sniffing. One took a lick, then a bite and the rest is rap history. Yolo was so impressed she called Casper immediately.

"Yolo? What the hell is that!" he yelled to be heard over the yelling.

"I found some puppies! Can I keep them?"

Chapter 19

Casper reluctantly allowed Yolo to keep her man-eaters. Like a good pet owner, she fed them men. It was amazing how many guys got in the car with her even after she told them she wanted to feed them to her dogs. All they wanted to know was if they could fuck afterwards. She said yes but that part was a lie.

Yolo was not just a murderer she was a big fan of murderers. She spent her free time researching murders around the globe. As usual, all that killer talk got her all hot and bothered so she went to the shower to relieve herself. Nothing spells relief like busting a good nut.

Casper walked into the den and freaked out when he saw the image on the screen. The face of a suspected killer was a man who was supposed to be dead. A man he paid good money to have killed.

"Is that the fuckin' guy? Tell me that that's not the fuckin' guy! How the fuck is this fuckin' guy alive when I paid good fuckin' money to have this fuck wacked," Casper demanded in one of his classic hissy fits. "Yolooooooo!"

Yolo heard the murder in his tone and came instantly. She jumped from the shower and rushed as fast as her orgasm wobbly legs would take her. The Baron twisted his lips and turned his head when the naked girl burst into the room.

"Yes?" she huffed breathless from the nut and sprint.

Sa'id Salaam

"Go into the city and kill his whole family. His grandmother, the girlfriend, cook the baby. Make it ugly. I want a blood bath! But...put some clothes on first."

Killing or no killing Yolo was all girl and wanted to look cute. She selected a short skirt and sexy heels. She was going into New York City after all. You never know who you might bump into. A matching pistol went in her designer purse and off she went. Once she got on the Long Island Expressway, she floored the SUV.

Killing Killa's family was just a taste. Casper figured that if he killed everyone around him, he would comply. Crazy right? He sent him out of town on a quick job so he could keep an eye on him. The only time he knew the man's whereabouts was when he was doing a job. A Richmond, VA mid-level dealer was about to die for absolutely nothing.

When Yolo reached the housing projects she was disappointed to find out the family was gone. The video of her holding Killa's son spooked him enough to send them into hiding. She did manage to murder a neighbor and four men who offered to run a train on her. At least the trip wasn't a total loss. Now it was time to report in.

Tell me they're all dead! Lots of little pieces! A real fuckin' mess!" Casper shouted greedily upon taking the call.

"No," Yolo pouted, poking her bottom lip out. "They were already in the wind when I got here. I'm on the way home now..."

"No! Go to the airport. You're going to Atlanta!"

148

Yolo literally caught the next thing smoking to the ATL. A Black Mob associate met her at the airport and offered her a choice of weapons. She chose a gun and a knife. A big sharp one.

Instead of going to a hotel Yolo was dropped off at a condo owned by the Black Mob. The same one Killa used. Used for sexing only because they did not live there. Killa and Kitty would stop by and fuck while Yolo watched on the security cameras. It was like he knew he was being watched and showed out.

Yolo was hot reliving some of the vigorous sex seeing in this same unit. She recalled when Killa bent Kitty over this same sofa and delivered back shots that echoed in the room. That was a fine time for Kitty to walk in with her mother.

"Well hello," Kitty's mom sang sweetly as she stepped inside the condo.

"Who the hell are you?" Kitty demanded not so sweetly. She often wondered why Killa refused to live in the plush condo instead of the hideout in the boondocks. Was she the reason? Did he have the next chick up in the spot?

"My name is irrelevant! Well, that's not my name, I mean...um, Yolo! I'm Yolo damn it," Yolo spat frustrated at her own confusion.

"Ok so Miss Yolo, what the fuck are you doing in my man's condo?"

Kitty kicked off her shoes so mama did the same. It wouldn't be the first time they had to whoop ass together. Only problem was Yolo wasn't the type to take an ass whooping. She pulled her gun, then pulled her knife, and pulled some real bullshit.

Gunshots to both women's knees sent them both to the plush carpet below. They howled from the gunshots but when Yolo got started with that knife! She cut them both up into twenty pieces apiece.

"Now comes the fun part!" the bloody girl cheered then began putting them back together mismatched. Kitty's head went on mom's torso and vice versa. Arms, legs, and feet all switched.

"K-I-L-L-A and Y-O-L-O," Yolo sang as she wrote the words in blood on the wall. Once she was done, she showered and changed.

Yolo was a girl and girls are nosey so she couldn't help but go through Kitty's phone. First stop was the gallery and pictures of her crush.

"Mm, mm, mmph!" she proclaimed seeing Killa in various poses. Then came the dick pics. "Mm, mm, mmph!"

"Aww," Yolo moaned when she read a text from Killa proclaiming his love for her. "He said he loves...wait," Yolo said then stopped since Kitty's ears were on her mother's head. She went over to the mismatched head and relayed the message. She shrugged and texted back, 'at the condo.'

His reply of being on the way sent her scrambling from the condo. She didn't go far though. Just to an adjacent building to wait. When Killa arrived, she watched him through the high-powered scope of a high-powered rifle.

"Our boy is here," Yolo said to Casper via Bluetooth. She felt her panties soak on sight but was still ready to fire. "Let me end this."

"No! Not yet! He has to make penance first," Casper whined. "Let him come to us!"

"Ok," Yolo moaned and put down the gun. She hung up the call and shook her head. "He gon' come to us alright, and kill us all."

Chapter 20

Casper was really foolish enough to think that he was safe. He actually believed that Killa would never be able to find their compound. He thought the gated mansion was a fortress against all evil. Evil perhaps, but not Killa. He was worse than evil and he was angry.

Yolo on the other hand knew he was coming. The question wasn't if, it was when. In her twisted mind, life was nothing more than waiting to die. After all, death is the only certainty in life. Until the inevitable came she entertained herself playing in her vagina while watching Killa's porn.

Casper didn't keep much security besides the tall gates and vicious dogs. The now fully-grown man-eaters were kept slightly hungry to make them even more dangerous. Yolo cut their diet to two men a week and they were starved. Anyone coming over that gate was dog food, literally.

"Hey big fella," Killa greeted warmly as he lined one of the dogs up in his scope. The large canine cocked his head and turned as if he heard the sniper in the woods.

Killa fired, exploding his head with a silent round. The next dog came over to investigate and his nosey ass got the same. The last dog seen all it needed to see and took off. Tried to anyway, because Killa gunned it down as well. I'm not sure if all dogs go to heaven but wherever they're going, they all went together.

After scanning the home and grounds through the scope for several minutes, Killa was ready to make his move. He broke the sniper rifle back down and put it back in his bag. He pulled a large pistol and made his approach. Killa had hopped many a wrought iron fence growing up in New York City. The athletic goon had no problem getting over the gate. Assuming correctly that no one would use a moving truck for a getaway; he ignored it and rigged the other vehicles with explosives. This way if he didn't make it, they wouldn't either.

Killa slipped gun first into the doggy door in the kitchen. Once the coast was clear, he climbed all the way in and stood erect. He scanned the house with his eyes and ears as he inched forward. Suddenly the slurpy sound of sloppy dick sucking caught his ear. He quietly crept forward and found his man.

"Sorry to interrupt but..." Killa announced and shot the pretty blonde girl giving the Baron head right in her blonde head. The large man came as close to speaking then than any time in his life. The disappointment of an interrupted blowjob was etched on his face. That shit hurt, hurt deep.

The room was quiet as everyone tried to figure out what just happened and was about to happen. Casper went limp instantly inside of his brunette hooker's head. She took the opportunity to leave.

"I guess I better go. I see you boys have business," she said politely.

"I think you should go too," Killa agreed just as politely and sent her with her friend with a head shot.

"Black Mob," Killa said with a sarcastic scowl as he approached the Baron. The Baron looked over to Casper for help and got none. "You killed my woman? Went after my family?"

The Baron just sat there mute as ever, which further infuriated the killer. Killa pumped a round into his knee to see if that would get him talking. It didn't, but he did howl to the highest heavens. The guttural moan echoed throughout the large house.

"Huh?" Yolo asked when the screech reached her. It was a rhetorical question that she already knew the answer to. "He's here!"

There was no time to get dressed so she donned her vest and pulled the dreadlock wig on her head. She grabbed the closet pistol and rushed into battle. Crept actually, as she tiptoed towards the action.

"Nothing to say?" Killa asked cocking his ear towards the man. When he still didn't reply Killa shot his other knee. He caught the help creeping towards the door and sent a slug his way too.

"So sorry!" Casper blurted out from the pain of being shot in his ass cheek. When he spoke, the cat was out of the bag.

"You?" Killa asked with a confused frown. He looked back and forth between the large man and the man with the voice that called the shots. The voice that made the threats. Killa was as smart as a rocket scientist and quickly figured it out. He couldn't help but laugh, "Black Mob."

"I am!" Casper said suddenly smug. "He's my flunky, the black face of the Black Mob!"

"Looks like you're gonna need a new face," Killa growled and took off the Baron's old face with a shot. He didn't know Casper's cavalier attitude was courtesy of Yolo's arrival. Killa didn't see her but he sure felt her. She raised her gun and shot the intruder in the middle of his back.

"Ugh!" Killa groaned from the impact. He spun and fired back. He and Yolo traded shots, testing the veracity of their bulletproof vests. They both back peddled from the impact until they both fell on their asses.

Both killers jumped to their feet and raised their guns. They both pulled their trigger and got the same results. Their guns clicked harmlessly from lack of bullets. Killa quickly exchanged the empty clip for a full one while Yolo twisted her lips. She didn't have an extra clip.

"I shoulda shot you in that pretty face," she quipped.

"I'm damn sure about to shot you on yours," Killa replied noticing not only that she was pretty but naked as well.

"He's getting away," Yolo said hoping to divert his attention long enough to make a break. If that didn't work, she still had a trick up her sleeve and she didn't even have on a shirt. She did have a brand new unused vagina though. That's gotta be good for something.

"He won't get far," he announced just before the sound of his car exploding reached them. "Not in one piece anyway."

"Good! He's dead. I just followed orders, just like you. It's over," Yolo shrugged as if it were really just that simple. Seeing he wasn't moved, she made her next sales pitch.

"Yo, we got ten thousand kilos of Columbian cocaine out in that truck. It's worth millions!" she offered seductively.

"Bitch they haven't printed enough money for me to spare you. After what you did to my woman!" Killa growled and delivered a backhand like something out of YUNG PIMPIN'. The blow knocked her down causing her legs to spread slightly.

"Mmm, that turns me on," Yolo purred. She saw his eyes dart between her legs and parted them a little more. "I guess I'm dead so at least fuck me first. Don't let me die a virgin."

"A what?" Killa frowned at the foreign word. It actually took him a second to recall what it meant but that didn't make sense. "Get the fuck outa here!"

"I'm for real! Just cuz I kill people don't mean I'm a hoe," she shot back indignantly then softened. "I was saving myself for my husband but don't look like I'ma live long enough to get one."

Yolo pushed the issue by rubbing her bare box. She then lifted her wet fingers to show off. The look of pure awe on his face urged her on. She crawled over and pulled his dick from his pants. It grew long and hard in her hot mouth and she knew she had him. Until he shot his knee up and knocked her over.

"You wanna get fucked? Well I'm about to fuck you!" he growled. There would be no tenderness; he intended to punish her before she died.

Killa snatched Yolo's legs open by an ankle and forcefully plunged inside. He actually felt her hymen give way when he pushed past it. A thin coat of blood confirmed her claims of chastity.

"Shit! Shit! I love you!" Yolo screamed from the searing pain.

Killa ignored her screams and pounded away. It was a consensual rape designed to punish, not please. Somewhere along the way pleasure mixed with the pain causing Yolo to moan.

"Mmm baby this is yours we should be together. Imagine our kids!" she wailed. Killa just kept on pounding. He wanted to bust a nut so he could kill her. His gun was still in hand for the moment he came.

"You 'bout to make me cum," she whined as the sensation increased.

Her proclamation of pleasure pushed Killa to pound harder. He was determined to get off then off her before she could. He won that race but just barely. He pushed right up against her cervix and exploded. Yolo came a second later with a soft whimper.

"Stupid bitch," Killa growled and shot her in the back of her dreadlocked head. She fell face first and he fired again. "Got some good pussy though."

He used a throw pillow from the sofa to clean the blood, semen and pussy juice from his still erect dick and tucked it away. Then a slow smile spread as he surveyed the carnage in the room. The Baron was missing his face with a prostitute at his feet. Ironically, the blonde still had her month open. A true cocksucker till the end. Casper's date was also stretched out and he was in a hundred chunks in the driveway.

"The fuck I'ma do with ten thousand keys?" he pondered as he pulled the truck from the house. He snapped his fingers as his cousin Cameron Forest came to mind. It was time for the return of the Dope Boy.

Chapter 21

When Killa shot Yolo, the bulletproof wig saved her life. She was merely knocked unconscious by the impact. Additionally she had a hairline skull fracture and concussion. She lay there for an hour until she realized that she wasn't dead. Dead people don't feel pain but she hurt like hell. "Ow," Yolo moaned like a girl as her eyes fluttered open. The events of the day slowly came to mind and explained the pain between her legs. "Mmm, that was good baby. I love you but I still gotta kill you..."

Yolo finally took to her feet but a dizzy spell sat her back down. She couldn't help but nod in approval at the dead guests around the room. Not knowing if Killa would come back, she knew she had to get out of there. It took all she had to make it to her room to dress. She pulled a few clothing items into a bag along with twenty something thousand dollars in cash she kept in her room. There was over a million dollars in the house but it would have to wait. Last but not least, she grabbed a gun.

Yolo climbed into her truck and inserted the key. A last second glance upward saved her life. Had she not seen Casper's foot in the tree she would have turned the ignition and joined him. Luckily, for Yolo, she had used the same device many times and was able to disarm it.

"Oh my," she whined as she pulled onto the expressway. The SUV swerved and crossed lanes as she fought to stay awake. Seeing a sign for a hospital at the next exit, she gave up and pulled off. With her last bit of energy, Yolo walked into the emergency room and passed out.

Yolo felt the oddest sense of Déjà vu when she awoke hours later. She reached up and felt the stitches in the bald spot shaved in her head. She frowned the frown of recognition at the elderly lady buzzing around the room. The nurse saw she was finally awake and told her off.

"Mm hm you frowning at me but you should be frowning at whatever man bust your head! You girls kill me letting these men beat you up. Shoot I wish I would let some man beat on me! My daddy ain't even put his hands on me!"

"I never met my dad. My mom either," Yolo admitted sadly. She somehow felt connected to the woman and spoke freely. "I had a foster mom but she tried to sell me so I killed her. Cut her up into little pie…"

"Girl you delirious," Nurse Marquita said placing the back of her hand on her forehead despite the thermometers. "What's you name girl?"

"Yolo. Yolo Jackson."

The nurse snatched her hand away and stumbled backwards upon hearing the name she named a dead baby so many years ago in this same hospital. She shook her head 'no' but she could clearly see the face of the blue baby she pulled feet first into the world.

"What?" Yolo asked, fearful from her strange reaction.

"Girl you are not going to believe this but…" Marquita began and told her about her arrival in the world. She told her about her mom, her birth, and especially the nasty ass doctor who wanted to let her die.

"Where is that doctor now?" Yolo asked with murder in her voice.

"Child his old ass done retired. Somewhere down in Florida. Never mind him. Tell me about you. How was your life?" the nurse asked curiously.

"You are not going to believe this but…" Yolo began and laid out her life story up until that point. The nurse was dubious at first at the tall tales but she spoke with such detail and clarity she had no choice but to accept it.

"That needs to be a book! No, a movie!" Marquita cheered when she reached the end of her narrative. "Get dressed and hurry!"

"Where am I going? To jail?" Yolo asked feeling as close to fear as possible for her. For the first time in life, she was too weak to fight.

"No. I'm gonna do what I should have done 21 years ago. Take you home!"

Yolo recovered quickly and comfortably in Marquita's small home. The two women developed a mother/daughter bond since both were deprived of that. She taught Yolo to cook real meat, not babies, and other domestic duties girls should know. Things were great for the first two months until disaster struck.

"Girl what's wrong with you?" Marquita asked seeing Yolo turn as green as the bell peppers she was sautéing to go in the lasagna.

"I don't know, I... " she replied then rushed over to the garbage can and threw up. "The smell made me nauseous."

"You better not be!" the woman demanded.

"Better not be what?" Yolo asked naively. She may have been green but the nurse knew the symptoms all too well.

Marquita drove Yolo to the drug store fussing the whole way. She bought four different pregnancy tests and fussed the whole way home. Yolo peed on four different stick and got one same result.

"Please tell me it ain't by the man who bust your head!" she demanded when she saw the four positive test.

"Actually he shot me in my head but yeah. That's the only time I ever had sex."

"Well you made your bed and you gon' lie in it! We don't do no abortions in this house! Your mom didn't abort you did she? No she didn't!" the childless woman yelled. She was set to retire herself and what better to keep her busy than a baby?

"I don't want an abortion," Yolo admitted to Marquita and herself. "He has other kids, two."

"Well I hope he can take care of them because…" she said entering another tirade that Yolo missed. She was too busy making plans for her child to be Killa's only child. A mischievous grin spread on her face as she plotted.

Killa kept the business phone supplied by the Black Mob more out of nostalgia than anything. He still had pictures of the Baron and Casper, well a piece of Casper that he got a kick out of. He kept it charged so he could view the pictures and get a good laugh. But when it rang...

"What wrong?" Sincerity asked seeing his startled reaction.

"Nothing," he replied and regained his South Bronx cool. He frowned at Casper's number and took the call. "Yeah?"

"Hey bae, it's me Yolo. Or should I say baby momma? Anyway I was watching animal planet and I saw when a lion takes over the pride he kills the baby lions so the girl lions will go in heat and just have his babies so I said I'll..."

"You're dead! I killed you?" He recalled shooting her twice in her head. At near point blank range to boot.

"Nuh uh, my wig was bullet proof silly! Anyway I'm in Philly waiting on little Xavier to get out of school, by the way he is a cutie, so I can kill him. Next I have to kill little Rico so our child can be your only child," Yolo rambled as only Yolo could.

"Listen carefully; I need you to meet me..."

"Oops gotta go. Talk to you later, bye-bye."

"I gotta go to Philly!" Killa shouted as he tore off towards the door. He was already in his vehicle by the time Sincerity processed the statement.

Killa ignored all traffic signs and laws as he sped down 95 south. He had set a new second when he pulled into the city of brotherly love, driven by fatherly love. He pulled to a screeching halt in front of his son's school and hopped out. He breathed a sigh of relief seeing his smiling son walk out. The little boy barely knew him but he planned to kidnap him to keep him safe.

"Hey little man," Killa smiled down at his miniature self. The little boy looked up, smiled, and then died. Yolo shot him with a high-powered rifle from a rooftop several blocks away.

"One down, one to go," she said proudly after his little head exploded.

****

"Beat it little nigger bird," a fussy old man cursed from his park bench. Ever since Doctor Mayes retired to Florida, he came to feed the birds in the park. Every day a black crow would swoop in and grab as much bread as he could and fly off. He was indeed a little nigger bird.

The doctor looked up and frowned at the young pregnant black woman waddling towards him. In his long career back in New York, he deliberately botched plenty of births. Some babies died, some had debilitating injuries. He gave a few unsuspecting women abortions and sterilized a few as well.

"Good morning doctor," the young lady sang with a pleasant smile. She extended what looked like a Polynesian lei.

"Oh ok," Doctor Mayes grumbled and leaned forward so she could place the flowers over his head. He figured if he went along she would leave him alone. Run off and give birth to a little nigga or nigglette and drink malt liquor. Twerk, talk loud, tell all its business online and whatever else niggers loved so much. Figured wrong because it was he who was leaving.

"Oh bye-bye," Yolo sang, waving her free hand and hitting the switch with the other. The D.C. 2000 snapped closed and popped off his fat racist head. She collected her device and headed back to New York. She still had one more kid to kill.

Chapter 22

The Head or Tail strip club in Baltimore, Maryland was the most ratchet spot in the city. You could actually order a blowjob to go along with your malt liquor. The low budget dudes who hung out there spent more money with the in-house weed man than on the so-called strippers. The raggedy rundown women were reduced to blowjobs in the booths or back shots bent over a chair.

Ironically, this same club was once the shit, until Yolo came along and murdered the manager. It was the former headquarters of the Menendez brothers, but the Lovely Little Lunatic killed them too. There were no blowjobs or back shots being peddled that night.

That night there was a meeting being held for the head nigga in charge of Black Mob operations in every city. They along with their second in command were summoned for the emergency meeting. Once they arrived, the lieutenants were shuttled off to a separate location. It was for bosses only.

"So...why you got us all here? Where's The Baron? Where's Casper?" Big Bang snarled at the host Big Rock.

Big Bang ran the Black Mob interest down in Atlanta, Georgia. They called him bang because that's the sound his guns made. The big was because he was a big motherfucker. Big Bang, how ironic.

"Fo' real though!" a dyke called Daddy Mack frowned.

She tried to look hard but was still a pretty woman despite the mean mug. She and her cousin and fellow carpet muncher Lil' Man represented the Black Mob in New Orleans. That meant despite vaginas those two were very dangerous men/women. They climbed to the top of their city over the dead bodies of their competition. It's hard to compete when you're dead.

"Ain't nobody seen or heard from Baron n'dem in some months," Redd from Birmingham added.

"That's why we're all here," Big Rock began, as he addressed the heads of state from Houston, LA, Miami, and everywhere else.

"Hole up...what's that smell?" Mason wanted to know. The Detroit captain frowned as he sniffed the air. Mixed in with pussy, smoke, sweat, blood, and semen was another familiar fragrance that he couldn't quite place. Too bad for him.

"This is a strip club!" Rock shot back. "You smell pussy. Ain't that right Daddy Mack?"

"I smell pussy, dirty pussy, but pussy," the pretty stud replied in a forced husky voice.

"So where the hoes at? Where the party?" T-Rock from Orlando asked.

In an odd twist of fate, he had become a pussy hound just like the man he replaced. Rock shook his head at the inane question and went on.

Yolo

"The Baron and Casper are dead. Sun-Sun informed me and I personally went to see what was left," he advised with the New York captain nodding in agreement.

"A-yo, that nigga Casper was hanging from a tree! Baron was missing his whole face son!" Sun-Sun said in typical animated New York fashion. It almost sounded like he was rapping.

"Yolo too?" the Newark boss asked fearfully. He remembered when she hit the Brick City like a ton of bricks.

"Please tell me that crazy bitch is dead too!" C-P pleaded.

Yolo had torn through Phoenix like a tsunami, knocking down buildings and grown men in her path.

"No, she's still alive. The man named Killa killed The Baron. She had to be down with him for him to spare her," Rock surmised.

"So shit, I can keep their cut I been holding then!" Daddy Mack announced.

She like everyone else held on to the share when no one came to collect. She like everyone else had brought it along to Baltimore. Over twenty million dollars waited across town with their second in commands.

"Each man for himself!" Redd cheered.

"No! Everything stays the same. Same structure, same strength. We separate and we lose our connect. The Chinese fuck with us because of our unity," Rock reminded. "We just need a new leader."

"Who, you?" Bang huffed indignantly.

"I nominate me," Fresh from Houston suggested. "I got the ports where the work comes in. Got transportation, muscle..."

"Why not me? I got the biggest team! Manhattan, the Bronx, Staten Island," Sun-Sun rambled, stating his case. Big Rock smiled seeing it going pretty much like he'd figured it go.

"You? Yeah right!" Daddy Mack laughed cutting Sun-Sun off. "Nigga, I got a pussy and still got bigger balls than you!"

"She...he do!" Hawk from Miami co-signed. "You'se a bitch."

"Gentlemen, gentlemen," Rock said raising his hands along with his voice to regain control. Once he had it, he continued. "The man for the job has to be extremely violent to keep order. Think Mr. Grimsly. Unfortunately, some of us will die in this process. It is what it is. I nominate myself, but we'll take a vote. I'll send in the girls while you guys mull it over."

The moans and groans started before Big Rock was all the way out of the room. It came to a curious halt when the girls walked in from the dressing room. The beat up dancers limped, hobbled, and staggered into the club. Daddy Mack twisted her face up at the ugly bunch, but then again, she didn't have a dick. The rest of the men selected one because a nut is a nut.

Rock held his breath as he walked briskly through the girls' dressing room. Actually a fish would have held its breath if it walked through the funky room. It didn't smell like fish. It smelled like a vagina that a fish swam up and died in.

Once out in the alley, he hopped in his car and drove to the new strip club. That one was scheduled for demolition soon.

"Sup boss," Bull asked as Rock walked into Club Platinum where the meeting for the second in command was being held. They were all about to be promoted.

"Everything is everything," he replied and nodded at the lively festivities. The rules were relaxed for the evening, which meant sex in the champagne room.

Daddy Mack's cousin, Danny Boy, didn't make it that far. She was eating peaches out of Peaches' pussy right at her table. Lil' Redd giggled as he played in Chili's box. It squished and squashed all over his fingers. Good stuff.

"Once y'all get your rocks off we can get started," Rock announced.

Hands, hips, and lips all went into overdrive to speed things along. A few minutes later Rock stood center stage and addressed the meeting. "I'd like to start out with a gift."

"A gift? You mean that wasn't it?" Sosa from Detroit asked out of breath from busting a nut.

"Nah, ol' Vanilla is just an appetizer. As you know, The Baron and Casper have been MIA. And I know y'all held on to their money. Wouldn't want Yolo to come see about you," he said and watched eyes open wide in fear. "Well, keep it! The Baron is dead, Casper is dead, and I'm the new boss of the Black Mob."

"Is that right?" Saleem asked grabbing his phone. "Let me see what Sun-Sun got to say about this!"

"Congratulations on your promotions. You are all the new bosses of your respective cities," Rock went on as if the New Yorker hadn't even spoken.

"We can keep the money?" Danny Boy asked cocking her head dubiously. She knew that they brought over three million from the Big Easy. "What about Daddy Mack?" she asked proving that money was thicker than blood.

"They…"Rock said pulling his phone out, but was interrupted by Sun-Sun on Saleem's speakerphone.

"A-yo! What the fuck you got going on?" Sun-Sun demanded.

"Have been fired," Rock continued and pressed Send, sending a signal to detonate the hundred pounds of Sentex that Mason smelled. He should have trusted his judgment and run up out of there instead of sticking his cock in some cockeyed girl. She got blown up right along with him and everyone else.

"What about Yolo?" Pep wanted to know. He had once been at the bottom of the totem pole in Houston until Yolo started chopping off heads.

"We believe she is in cahoots with Killa. They are a threat to us all. If the Chinese find out we have these loose ends they will cut us off. That's why I put a five million dollar bounty on them."

"Five million! Each?" was asked.

"Each. Catch them together and that's an easy ten mil," Rock replied.

"It may be ten million," Sosa said and added, "But ain't nothing easy about that!"

Yolo

Chapter 23

"Hey pretty girl," Yolo greeted warmly to the pretty girl in the mirror. She was smiling brightly so she smiled back. Not many people dressed up to make a phone call, but she is a lunatic after all.

She went through the ritual almost daily, but always chickened out. Not that day though. This was the day she was going to call her boo. After one last check of her lip-gloss, she held her head up triumphantly and made the call.

"We got activity! On both lines!" a high-tech technician said when his high-tech equipment detected activity on the Black Mob phones used by Killa and Yolo. His elation was short lived when the signals started bouncing around the globe. He knew good and damn well she wasn't in Afghanistan and Killa definitely wasn't sitting next to him.

Killa stared at the phone for a minute to make sure it wasn't his imagination. He put a tracer program on it as well so he could trace and kill Yolo if she ever called. Reluctantly, he took the call.

"Yeah?"

"Hey bae, it's me," Yolo barely managed to get by the broad smile stretching her pretty face. "Still mad at me?"

"Mad? Nah, why would I be mad?" he asked trying to trace the call.

Sincerity's eyes popped open hearing his female friendly voice. It was a far cry from the gruff barks he used when speaking to men.

"Miss me?" Yolo asked and almost ducked. She crossed her fingers and held her breath hopefully.

"Of course I miss you," Killa said causing his girl to pop up in bed like she was spring loaded.

"Who? Who you miss?" she barked. "Nuh uh, don't try to cover the receiver! Who you talking to?"

"Chill, it's her!" Killa growled through clenched teeth.

"Ugh, I see that bitch is with you. My fault, I should have killed her when I had the chance," Yolo pouted. "I have to hurry and kill them before the baby comes. I don't want anything to get in our way. Ok, bye!"

"Damn baby! How am I 'posed to catch her and you playing jealous girlfriend!" he shot in frustration. "You act like I'm tryna fuck the broad. I'm tryna kill her!"

"Fuck her again you mean! Oh, and I am a jealous girlfriend. Whenever we catch up to the chick I'm gon' be the one to pull the plug on her ass!"

"You?" Killa chuckled in amusement. "She's a little tougher than Shane. Trust me; you are not ready for Yolo."

"I'm Karate Joe's only daughter, trust me, Yolo ain't ready for me!"

****

"Mm hm, who got you all in your feelings?" Marquita asked as Yolo sulked into the room still holding the satellite phone.

The observant woman knew there was something special about the phone. Yolo kept it fully charged but never used it. No text, no calls, pokes, or likes. She now knew it was the link to her mysterious baby daddy. Curiosity was getting the best of her. The same curiosity that killed the cat and a whole bunch of other nosey people.

"Once I have this baby I'll have him all to myself," Yolo convinced herself.

It was the baby mama mantra recited all around the world by a million baby mamas before her. It proved true for 12, the rest are at the WIC office, alone.

****

"I don't mind coming you know. You certainly don't have to be shy around me. I brought you into this world, literally," Nurse Marquita reminded as Yolo prepared for her prenatal visit.

"I'm a big girl," she replied still in a funk.

The private girl hated being prodded and poked by doctors. The stirrups just added insult to injury. She did want a healthy child and put her reservations to the side and manned up.

"Well, ok…Guess I'll go to the market. Need anything?" the sweet little lady offered.

Yolo smiled warmly and declined with a kiss on her cheek. "See you later," she said and turned to leave.

Marquita was right behind her and they left in separate directions. A half hour later Yolo arrived at the out of the way clinic.

"Yolo Jackson," she huffed with her trepidation evident in her voice.

"What a pretty name," the receptionist cooed attempting to soothe her nerves. She wasn't the first young woman to visit the office all by her lonesome. "What does it mean?"

"It's Swahili for none of your damn business," she replied evenly, and then cracked a friendly half-smile.

"Well you're a little early...but we had a cancelation so you can be seen now if you'd like," the woman offered unfazed by the rude remark. She certainly wasn't the first young woman to visit the office with a fly ass mouth either.

"I like," Yolo quipped but took a little off this time. Yolo followed the directions down the hall to an examination room. She saw a clean gown on the exam table and slipped into it leaving her panties on. No sooner did she climb on the table did the door open and in walked a young black guy.

"I'm supposed to have a woman doctor!" she insisted.

"Doctor yes, nurse no. Just gotta prep you before she comes in. Feet up please," he said pulling the stirrups into position.

"Man..." Yolo fussed as she complied. The gown stretched across her knees prevented her from seeing what was going on at the other end of the table. Good thing too.

180

Yolo

"Should have removed these," he said pulling her panties to the side. He whipped his phone out and began snapping pictures of the neatly shaved vagina. Using his fingers, he spread her labia to put a little pink in the pictures. He couldn't help himself and pushed his luck by pushing a digit inside her.

"Man," Yolo pouted at the intrusion.

"Damn, you tight!" he exclaimed feeling the hot box clamped around his finger.

"Excuse me?" she said trying to lift up and see what he was doing.

"Huh? Oh um...the doctor will be right in," he said scurrying from the room.

Yolo was still staring after him when the lady doctor walked in.

"Oh?" she declared surprised to see the patient in the gown and even more so in stirrups. "We're just doing an ultrasound today. You actually could have kept your clothes on."

"But the nurse..."

"Nurse! I wish they would send me a nurse. All I have is the receptionist Jen. Oh and Jason, the janitor," the doctor replied.

"Shole nuff! Is that right?" Yolo said realizing she had just been molested. Oddly enough, she wasn't even mad. Quite giddy in fact. Murder always made her happy and he was definitely going to get murdered.

"Everything looks great. Would you like to know the sex of your baby?" the doctor asked once it was visible on the screen.

"Um…" she though with a thoughtful frown. "Nah, surprise."

The doctor rambled on about sleep, rest, blah, blah, blah as Yolo rushed to put her clothes back on. Yolo missed most of it in her haste.

"Ok thanks, Doc," she said appreciatively as she accepted the huge prenatal pills and pamphlets. She was eager to get to her play date for the evening.

"Do you have a hobby? Something you enjoy doing?" the woman asked.

"Yeah…why?" Yolo asked curiously, stopping short of telling her what it was. Probably wouldn't have believed her anyway.

"Well, do it as much as you can. Happy mothers birth happy babies," she assured her. She'd just killed ol' Jason and didn't even know it. A huge grin spread on Yolo's face at the good news.

Yolo rushed out into the hallway and snapped her head left, right, and then left again like a child trying to cross the street. Except she wasn't looking for cars, she was looking for Jason.

The janitor stepped out of the janitor's closet on wobbly knees from just busting a nut. The pictures of the pretty pussy prompted him to pull on his penis. He couldn't wait until he got home. Most of the patients were older with rundown vaginas. A few looked like they could just stand up and let the baby drop out.

Yolo

He flinched when he saw Yolo like he wanted to run. He wouldn't have gotten too far on his rubbery legs. Luckily, Yolo flashed a smile at him that froze him in place. He went for it and smiled back as she approached. Sorta like the cheese in a mousetrap. Looks tempting, and then breaks your neck.

"I think you tricked me! You're not a real nurse, you just wanted to see my goodies," Yolo giggled like it was no big deal. As if she wasn't going to brutally murder the man.

"See I...um, no. But I'm going to back to school soon so I be tryna get some practice," he lied.

He was going to upload the pictures to a freaky social media site. It was dedicated to perverts like himself who took up skirt and hidden camera pictures of unsuspecting victims. The only practice he got was jacking off. The nasty bastard.

"Oh ok, that makes sense," she pretended. "Hey! Why don't I come to your house so you can get more practice? Really spend some time with my vagina."

"Really? Can I? Hell yeah!" Jason cheered just short of doing a back flip.

Instead, he whipped out a pen and paper and quickly scribbled down his address. He skipped happily down the hall after setting his date for the evening. The rest of his day dragged by dreadfully slow. Luckily, it was his last day on the job. Unluckily it was his last day on the planet.

****

Jason spent the last few hours of his life getting his tiny apartment tidy for his date. It would be the first time he had a girl over. A real girl that is since 'Suzie the Fluzie' was deflated and tucked away. After vacuuming, dusting, and cleaning the kitchen, he jacked off to Yolo's pictures once more. That was so he could last if he actually got lucky.

He wasn't the only one masturbating. Yolo was so excited about the impending murder that it made her wet. She squished into her room to relieve herself for the first time in a long time. She barely played with her love button before an orgasm shook her body.

"Fuck! Damn it man!" she fussed at the climax. It took the edge off, but now she really wanted to kill something. Good thing Jason came into her life and offered his in sacrifice.

"Let's see...Eenie, meenie, miney...mo!" she sang childishly as she selected a murder weapon from her collection of murder weapons.

A little .22 caliber revolver got the call. She picked it so she could shoot him quite a few times before he checked out on her. The larger guns were one shot, one kill, and what fun is that?

"And just where are you going all gussied up?" Marquita inquired when Yolo came out looking cute.

"I'm not...gussied," she giggled at the old timey compliment. Actually, she looked pretty in the knee length skirt and sandals, even with the baby bump in the middle.

"Well at least I don't have to worry about you getting pregnant," she cackled and cracked up at her own joke.

"Ha ha," Yolo said and leaned in to kiss her fleshy cheek.

A wide smile adorned the nurse's face as she watched the girl leave.

Meanwhile Jason was pacing like a caged lion as he waited for his date. He contemplated jacking off once more, making it the fourth of the day. Sounds excessive to you and me, but his personal record was 13; with his nasty ass. If he scored, he planned to brag far and wide. Most of his pervert friends didn't get much real pussy. Real pussy as opposed to hands and latex dolls that they referred to as pussy. The pictures of Yolo he'd uploaded earlier had made him the man.

"Yes, yes, yes!" he cheered when his doorbell rang. He pumped his fist, spun in a circle, and this time hit a backflip. He actually felt lightheaded when he pulled the door open and saw the pretty girl standing there. He took a deep breath and inhaled her girly smell.

"I sure hope you know how to eat pussy," she announced as she barged in past him. She marched over to the sofa and sat down. He blinked rapidly as she leaned back and pulled off her moist panties.

"I, I, I," Jason stuttered as he forgot all the words he ever knew.

"I, I, I hope t, t, that's a y, y, yes," Yolo teased. "Get over here!"

Jason closed the door and meekly complied. He came over and knelt before her vagina as if it was an altar. It wasn't, but it was nice and pretty so he leaned in and kissed it. Eating pussy is pretty much self-explanatory. He tuned into her hisses and moans and let them be his guide. When he twirled his tongue inside of her that was all she wrote. She tried to fight off the orgasm, which only made it worse. She came so hard the sofa moved.

"Fuck! You can eat some pussy!" she proclaimed. Jason just clamped down on her juice box and sucked it dry.

"So, how'd I do?" he asked eagerly with his face soaked with that good gravy. He figured it went well but he wanted to hear it again.

"You did great," she said patting him on his head like a puppy. "It was so good I almost hate to do this."

"Do what?" he asked curiously, as she dug into her purse. He didn't like the answer when she pulled the gun out and fired into his cheek.

The impact of the bullet knocked him back onto the table. He had no idea why she shot him, but now wasn't the time to ask. He rolled off the table and tried to make a run for it. He didn't make it far when a shot to his calf dropped him.

"Man that feels good! I haven't shot anyone in months," Yolo proclaimed as she stood and shot him again, again, and again, and then once more. The shots to his face and neck were all fatal.

By the time, the six shots were spent, so was he. His soul seeped out of one of the many holes she plugged in him. She stepped over his dead body and removed all traces of her ever being there.

Curiosity got the best of her so she went through his phone. She didn't find any pictures of his dick but recognized her vagina right off. She saw where it was uploaded and took a look.

"Not bad," she nodded at all the likes and comments her box got. On a whim, she took a picture of Jason and loaded that.

The caption read, "Hot Date!"

Chapter 24

The murder and sex only served to frustrate the goofy girl even more. She wanted to see her Killa and decided to do just that. Dressed comfortably in sneakers and sweats she packed a sniper rifle and set off to the Bronx. She had no idea if she would see him or not, but would settle for a shot at shooting at his girlfriend.

The lovely little lunatic literally packed a lunch since she intended to wait on a sighting. A fresh fruit salad for the baby and a turkey on rye for herself.

She got set up on a nearby rooftop and watched the projects through the scope of the high-powered rifle. It was the visual comings and goings of life in the projects. Boys played ball and slang dope while girls played coy while slinging ass. Pretty boring until a familiar face ambled by.

"Is that the fuckin' guy? Nah, can't be," she said when Doc appeared. Killa was supposed to have killed him twice over so no way he was still alive. Not after all the trouble, he got him into. "It is! It is that fucking guy!"

It sure was that fucking guy. Doc had already lost his mind but kidnapping Killa's grandmother was just fucking stupid. The project dwellers had long ago learned to leave the white people the hell alone. Fucking with them brought heat and nobody got time for that.

"What are you up to?" Yolo wondered aloud when he entered Killa's grandmother's building.

She got her answer a few minutes later when he came out with Grandma in tow. Yolo had held enough people at gunpoint to recognize the look on her face. She really got in her feelings when she saw the DC 2000 around her neck.

"Hey! Where'd you get that?" she moaned even though she couldn't be heard from her perch. Typical girl shit, mad because she wasn't the only one with the latest fashion in murder.

She had to shake it off quick if she wanted to keep up. Yolo packed her rifle into its case and rushed downstairs. Doc and Grandma had just pulled off when she reached the lobby. He had a good head start but she managed to catch them on the 159th Street Bridge heading over to Harlem.

They zig-zagged all over Manhattan then over to Queens. When they finally reached their destination, Yolo pulled her phone out.

Killa returned from his grandmother's apartment in a daze. Seeing his childhood friend with his head on crooked added insult to injury. Sincerity was on the verge of tears from the look of horror on his face.

"Bae, what?" she pleaded. "What happened?"

"Yolo took my grandmother," he assumed. He too figured Doc was dead so it had to be her. "That crazy bitch is going to kill her!"

"That's it! I'm going to kill her myself!" Sincerity vowed. "Only I'm not going to fuck her first! I'ma make sure she dead! I'ma...what are you doing?"

"Really?" he asked in response to the silly question. His stuffing clothes in a suitcase could only be one thing. "Packing. You and the boys are going to South America until this is over. I can't concentrate on her and worrying about you guys!"

Sincerity opened her mouth to protest until he shot her a glance that shut her mouth. That didn't mean she was going to listen, she just wasn't going to speak. Not then anyway. The girl was as dangerous as she was hardheaded. She sucked her teeth and helped pack clothes for the boys. Time paused when the Black Mob phone rang.

****

"Hey boss, she's using the phone," the tech told Big Rock when Yolo made a call. "She's calling him!"

"Trace it!" Rock yelled.

He wanted to be the one to kill them so he could keep the bounty for himself. Not to mention the awe that came along with killing the two most dangerous people on Earth.

"Shit, they're scrambled. Both of the phones are..." he began to explain but stopped when Rock shot him.

"Find me a new technician! I won't take no for an answer!" he demanded.

"You got it boss!" Bull said and jumped right on it. He didn't want to get shot too. Neither did the new tech so he traced both phones.

****

"Answer it!" Sincerity reminded Killa as he watched it ring. He snapped out of it and a mask of murder spread across his face.

"Where...is...she?" Killa demanded in a low growl that made the windows rattle. Yolo completely forgot what she was about to say when she heard it.

"Damn you got a sexy voice," she gushed feeling her maternity panties getting wet. "Where's who?"

"My grandmother, that's who!"

"Oh yeah, her," Yolo giggled then got serious. Halfway anyway. "I didn't take her but I know where she's at. I know you won't believe me so come see for yourself."

"Where?" he demanded and listened dubiously. He twisted his lips not sure what to think. This was the lunatic who killed his kid. He knew he couldn't trust her.

"Well, you believe her?" Sincerity questioned after he relayed the information. When he opened his mouth to answer the satellite phone began playing a vintage Biggie Smalls' song.

"Hello? Grandma?" Killa said eagerly upon answering.

"JFK. Gate 10," Diedra recited as if reading from a script. The line went dead immediately after she finished.

"She was telling the truth, but…if she didn't take her who did?" he wondered perplexed.

"Why the airport? That doesn't make no sense," Sincerity frowned.

"Makes perfect sense. I can't bring a gun pass check in. Shit I can't bring a pair of fingernail clippers!"

"You better shave your chin too, before they think you're a Muslim and tackle your ass!" She reminded him.

She didn't want him to have to go through what they put you know who through.

****

Yolo had the same dilemma when she followed Doc and Diedra to the gate. No way was she making it inside with a pistol in her purse. Doc was white and had no problem getting past security. Even with a DC 2000 around his hostage's neck. The TSA agent was too busy harassing a Muslim family to notice. Even went through the baby's diaper. All they found was baby shit.

Yolo had no intention of being unarmed and had to think quickly. She rushed back to the truck to see what she could use as a weapon. A wicked smile spread on her pretty face when an old lady rolled by in her wheelchair. The chair, the wig, and the oxygen tank were perfect.

"Excuse me ma'am," Yolo sang so sweetly you would think she was perfectly sane. Nothing could be further from the truth.

"Yes dear?" she replied just as sweetly and pulled her lips back to show off her new dentures.

"I'm gonna need your wig, wheelchair, oxygen tank, and your dress. Please."

The old lady chuckle at what she assumed was a joke. It wasn't. She found out rather quickly when Yolo wrapped the tubing from the tank around her neck and strangled her. Old girl put up a fight but lost. She kicked, squirmed, and struggled to no avail.

Yolo pulled her from the chair and stripped her to her old lady undergarments. She rolled the woman under her own care and donned her clothing. She had a disguise but still needed a weapon of some sort.

"Ah ha!" she exclaimed seeing the long knitting needles and yarn in her purse. She broke the sharp tip off and stuffed it up into the oxygen tank tubing. Once she turned the pressure up, she had a makeshift gun.

****

"Think, think, think," Killa ordered himself as he walked through the terminal. His eyes scanned everything he passed for a weapon. If worse came to worse, he would roll a newspaper tightly and use it as a club.

By the eighth terminal, he still hadn't found a weapon. By the ninth, he stopped by a newspaper stand. When he reached Gate 10 there was his grandmother, and to his surprise, Doc.

"Why won't anyone stay dead?" he asked painfully. The last time he saw his old friend he was in the room with a bloodthirsty killer.

"Well, Chief Flores stayed dead," he replied proudly. "And if you take another step, I'll hit the switch, and it's off with her head."

Killa saw the DC 2000 on his grandmother's neck and froze. He sank into a chair directly across from them and once more tried to figure out why there were there. Nothing came, so he asked.

"Then what? You just walk away? You kill her and I beat you to death right here," he vowed.

"You can try. It'll be an epic fight to the death! Two of America's most wanted killers fighting to the death in the middle of JFK airport!" Doc rambled like a madman.

"We..." Killa began until his train of thought was interrupted by an old woman rolling up in the aisle behind Doc's chair. Even in disguise, he recognized the Lovely Little Lunatic. The silly girl popped in the dead woman's dentures and smiled brightly. "What the fuck is going on here?"

Yolo looked straight ahead, as she rolled behind the babbling doctor. She turned the pressure to the max on the oxygen tank. Once she was directly behind him, she released the needle.

"What's going on here is..." Doc began until death told him to hush. The knitting needle entered the base of his skull and turned out the lights. He was going to stay dead this time.

"Bastard!" Diedra cursed and pulled the deadly device from her neck. As soon as she tossed it down, the bootleg model snapped shut. She rubbed her neck realizing just how close she came to losing her head.

"Even Steven? I saved your grandma. I was gonna kill her once but she wasn't home. So...anyway, we good?" Yolo asked with her crazy ass. She murdered his son so how could they ever be cool.

"Even Ste...not even close you psycho bitch!" he replied through clenched teeth. "I'm going to kill you the first chance I get."

"What about our baby?" she pouted, giggled, and pouted again. "Either way it'll be a beautiful death."

She cast a long loving glance at him while he stuck up his middle finger at her.

"Baby!" Diedra shrieked as the crazy girl in old lady clothes rolled away. "Boy, tell me you ain't got that girl pregnant!"

"Huh?" Killa said like he did when he was five. His grandmother knew the tone and shook her head as he led her away.

Chapter 25

"Where are we going?" Diedra demanded when Killa drove the wrong way to go to the Bronx. She turned and watched the sign for the Throgs Neck Bridge as they drove by it.

"We, nowhere. You, Sincerity, and the boys, South America. Not debatable," he barked.

Grandma poked her lip out but kept quiet. A storm was coming and he knew it.

****

"Team One, ready," a gunman announced into his walkie-talkie. He wasn't really a gunman per se since he was toting a grenade launcher.

"Team Two, ready," announced a voice in Long Island.

Big Rock smiled broadly and took a moment to bask in his impending victory. The new tech traced both Killa and Yolo's phones back to their homes. It was easy with the old tech lying dead at his feet.

"See what happens when you go against the mob?" Rock gloated. "Three, two, one…fire!"

Marquita had just walked to the large plate glass window to investigate the tinted out car that was parked out front. She pulled her glasses to her eyes to be sure she saw what she was seeing.

The grenade launcher made a 'poof' sound as it spit the high explosive projectile at her. It crashed through the glass and slammed into her chest. The round lifted her off her feet and carried her halfway across the room before exploding. The blast disintegrated the woman and demolished the house.

"The fuck is that?" Raheem asked when Team One pulled out his grenade launcher.

The man replied by shooting him and three more kids in the courtyard. He then aimed at Diedra's window and sent the explosive projectile inside. He reloaded and turned to Sincerity's building. Another 'poof' blew that apartment up as well.

Killa arrived minutes after they drove away.

****

"What now?" Killa frowned when he arrived at the chaotic scene. He saw the dead kids and destroyed apartments and became enraged. Knowing it had to be Yolo, he pulled out the Black Mob phone. "Crazy bitch!"

"Huh?" Yolo asked when she arrived at her blown up house. When she saw Marquita's car still in the driveway she knew she was gone. She too pulled her phone out in a rage. That had to be Killa's work.

****

"Boss! Both lines are active now! They're calling each other!" the technician yelled. To everyone's surprise, both targets survived the attacks.

"Hello?" both Killa and Yolo questioned when they heard a man's laughter on the line before they got a chance to even dial.

"I thought it was good-bye. I see I missed...this time," Rock chuckled dryly. "Won't miss next time."

"I, I, is th, th, this, B, B, Big Ro, Ro, Rock?" Yolo teased. She remembered how shook he was when she had to fly down and murder the Menendez brothers for him. "M, m, musta bought some b, b, balls online."

****

"Who the fuck was that?" Killa asked when Rock sucked his teeth and hung up.

"The same person who tracked our phones. Dump them and meet me where we just left," she said urgently.

Killa was a killer so he recognized what he was up against. Whoever found him had to know an old lady and small children lived in the blown up apartments. That spoke extreme violence, a language Killa was fluent in. Yolo did too, plus she was crazy.

The both dropped the now worthless phones where they stood and got back in their vehicles. An hour later, they both arrived back at JFK airport. They arrived back at the gate and found Doc still sleeping. It would be a long nap for the dead man.

"Just tell me who and where?" Killa growled.

"The Black Mob is who and they're everywhere. Way too many for you to handle by yourself. They'll never stop until we're both dead. They killed the only person I had left," Yolo pouted.

"I'm not letting them get away with this," he vowed. "Whatever I have to do, they are dying. Every city, every member."

"Well, protect me until I have this baby. Our...baby. I know all the players. Know how they move and where they lay their heads. You need me," she reasoned.

Killa pondered. He could only shake his head when he realized she was right. One can't go gunning for the mob half-cocked. "Every member in every city?"

"Yes, yes, yes!" Yolo sang, pranced, and cheered. Passerby's smiled warmly at the vibrant old lady. "Hells yeah! Me and you! Killa and Yolo! Let's give these fucks a beautiful death!"

"Whatever, come on," Killa said like a grumpy old man and turned to leave.

"Where are we going?" Yolo asked when he led her to the ticket counter.

"First stop, ATL. I gotta get guns. Lots and lots of guns."

"Ok, but I gotta get something from my truck," she pleaded.

"Leave it. We'll get another one when we get down south," Killa declined.

"We can't, they're one of a kind. The person that made them um…well, he died."

"You killed him didn't you," Killa twisted his lips and cocked his head.

"Ok, see, what had happen was…"

"Come on, we gotta hurry. The flight boards soon," he said cutting her off. He walked so briskly towards the parking deck she practically had to run to keep up.

"Hey! Slow down buddy. You got your mom running," a Good Samaritan protested as they walked. Killa glanced at his watch to see if he had enough time to kick his ass.

"Mind your business faggot," Yolo said pushing Killa along. It was her turn to lead once they got outside. She led the way to her SUV and hit the remote locks when they got close.

Yolo opened the door and pulled the old lady dress over her head. Killa shot a glance at her ass when she leaned into the truck. She grabbed what she came for, popped them in, then spun around, and cheesed.

"The fuck?" he grimaced at the platinum fangs. "Why doesn't that surprise me? Come on."

"Wait! One more thing," she protested and went back into her vehicle.

This time Killa deliberately turned his head so he wouldn't look at her ass. She pulled her dreadlocked wig on and twirled around.

"Mi now ready to get 'pon di plone."

Two hours later the plane landed in Atlanta. Killa hadn't noticed he'd gone to sleep until he woke up with Yolo on his shoulder. He couldn't help notice how peaceful and calm she looked. If someone were to see her at that moment, they wouldn't believe she was the vicious murderer that she was. Killa knew though, knew all too well.

"Get up!" he barked and nudged her off his shoulder.

"Huh? Oh," she replied in confusion from being snatched from her slumber. She practically had to run to keep up as he rushed through the terminal.

A well-placed call ahead had a rental car waiting for their arrival. Bigs also rented a hotel room for him but forgot his special instruction.

"So, who runs the Mob in Atlanta? He's the first to go," Killa asked as they rode along 285.

"Big Bang, he's a real killer," Yolo replied cracking them both up. He might have been a killer but was a Girl Scout compared to the occupants of the car. "A real show off. Loves to floss, always in the limelight."

"Then that's how he's going to die...in the limelight," he replied.

"Actually The Limelight is a club...but, that works too," Yolo giggled girlishly. "I'm gonna stick out like a sore thumb with this," she said rubbing her belly.

"Nah, you won't. You're not going. First kill is on me. I called it."

****

"Sup Killa, who dis?" Bigs wondered when he opened the door and saw Yolo standing next to Killa. His eyes zeroed in on her round belly. Dudes don't tote pregnant girls around unless...

"Sup yo," Killa replied in defeat. "This is..."

"Yolo," Yolo spoke up before he could come up with a fake name.

"Well hello Yo...the Yolo? The craz...eh...thee Yolo?" the big man shuddered in fear.

"I prefer Lovely Little Lunatic over crazy bitch, but yes, I am she," she sang quite pleased with herself.

"And..." Shawn grimaced at her baby bump.

"His," she replied and hooked her arm under Killa's.

"Get off me," Killa grumbled and pulled away.

Big Shawn led them straight into the showroom since that's what they were there for. He waited for the usual reaction people gave when entering the showroom but didn't get it. Yolo was no stranger to guns and ammo.

"Cool," was as excited as she got when she saw the boxes of grenades. She picked two up and juggled them while Killa toyed with the laser sight on a pistol.

The empty table that served as a shopping cart was slowly filled with murderous devices. Guns, bombs, knives, scopes, and silencers were added. They were almost done when one final object caught Killa's eye.

"What's this?" he asked holding it up.

"Um…a hack saw? You know, for cutting metal. I forgot the combination to a lock and had to cut it off," he explained. He frowned when Yolo and Killa smiled brightly at each other. "What?"

"Big Rock!" they answered together.

"Saving the best for l, l, last," Yolo giggled.

"What's up with this Big Bang cat?" Killa asked ready to mark the mark off his list.

"Nothing. He's dead. Word is he and every other Black Mob leader got killed at a meeting. Fat runs the show in the A now," Bigs explained.

Sometimes people are called by nicknames that don't really fit. A six foot three inch 280-pound dude is called Tiny. Or a chick goes by Precious and she's really worthless. This was not one of those times.

Fat was a fat motherfucker. The five foot five inch man tipped the scales at almost 400 pounds. His legs were actually bowed under the pressure of all that weight. He breathed with loud gurgling sounds from all the phlegm and fat in his throat. Still, he was a dangerous man who would rather have you killed than wonder if you could be trusted or not. Who's more trustworthy than a dead man? They're not saying shit.

"He's the opposite of Bang. An introvert," Yolo stated.

"Well that changes the dynamics. I'll take some of that," Killa said pointing at a box of plastic explosives. "Time to bake ol' Fat a cake."

"Cash or charge?" Bigs wanted to know of the twenty thousand dollar total. He handed over the card key to their hotel room.

"I'll transfer it later. I need to hit the room and get a shower and a nap," Killa replied and hit the door. Yolo smiled and waved as she left behind him.

A short drive later, they arrived at an extended stay hotel. It was filled with visiting workers and other professional transient families. The innocuous couple would fit right in.

"We'll head out to get clothes and other stuff when I wake up," Killa said over his shoulder as he led the way to the room.

"Ok babe," Yolo said happily.

Killa stopped dead in his tracks at 'babe' to protest, but blew it off and continued walking.

"Here we are," he announced opening the door. "Oh no!"

"Oh yes!" Yolo cheered at the lone bed that made him sad.

Killa was too tired to protest so didn't. Instead, he kicked his shoes off and climbed on the bed. He yawned once, blinked twice, and fell fast asleep. Yolo climbed on the bed and joined him in slumber land.

Chapter 26

It doesn't matter what position a man and woman go to sleep in in the same bed because they will always wake up cuddled up. They could start off on opposite sides but come morning she'll be snuggled up in his arms. It's only natural since men are the protectors and maintainers of women. This is also how a lot of blurred lines get crossed. Go to sleep in the friend zone and be lovers by dawn.

Not Killa though, he detested Yolo. He was the first to wake and found her round ass pressed up against his morning wood. To make matters worse, his arm was draped protectively over her with his hand on her belly. He could feel the baby moving around inside.

"Get off me," Killa muttered and rolled away. He planted his feet on the floor and got up.

"Man," Yolo pouted missing the embrace instantly. This was the first time she had ever spent the night with a man. He was also the only man she had sex with, the result of which was currently moving around inside of her belly.

Yolo looked into the mirror facing the bathroom and watched him pee. He then stripped and stepped into the shower. She took the opportunity to relieve her bladder as well.

"Get out!" Killa shouted from under the steamy water.

"I gotta pee," she replied and did just that. "I'll go get us some food, ok babe?"

"Whatever. Just don't flush the toi...ow!" he howled as the water turned ice cold from her flush.

"Oops, sorry," she giggled. She watched his silhouette through the flimsy shower curtain as she washed her hands.

"Just don't get hit by a car, or fall off a cliff, or eaten by a lion," Killa called behind her as she left the room.

****

"What to get? What to get?" Yolo pondered as she cruised the aisles of the local grocery store. It would be the first meal she cooked for her man and wanted it to be special. In the end, she filled the basket with typical breakfast food.

Killa was on the bed talking on the phone when Yolo returned to the room.

"Honey, I'm home," she sang with a giggle.

Killa rolled his eyes and kept on talking. Yolo blew him a kiss and went into the kitchenette area and got to work.

"Bigs came through!" Killa announced cheerfully when he hung up. "We got a homeboy who can get me next to this Fat bastard."

"That's great, honey," she sang and cracked an egg into a bowl. Half the shell fell in and she fished it out with her fingers.

"You sure you know what you're doing?" he wanted to know.

"Yes! I'm an excellent cook!" she defended herself.

"Is that right? What's your best dish?" Killa asked twisting his lips.

"Bab...um...eggs!" Yolo lied. Her best dish was broiled baby, or baby kabobs, or baby back ribs, or baby burgers...

A few minutes later, she presented a passable plate of scrambled eggs, turkey bacon, and hash browns. She tried to put a little switch in her ass as she went to the bathroom. It was wasted because Killa dug into his food. He paid her no attention, but she didn't believe him. She ducked under the shower and got clean.

"I need some clothes," Yolo announced wet and naked as she emerged from the bathroom. Killa was still eating and almost choked when he looked up.

"Huh?" he asked confused by her firm thighs. He zeroed in on her crotch with a couple days growth of hair. Then her round belly with a dark line running from her navel to her box. Her breasts were full and heavy.

Lunatic or not, she was lovely.

"Put some clothes on," he barked from embarrassment.

"That's what I said. I don't have none," she whined.

"Well, put on what you had and let's hit the store!"

"Ok!" she clapped then bent over to pick up her pants since she had his full attention.

****

"You like this, bae?" Yolo asked holding a maternity shirt up for his approval.

"Stop calling me bae!" he barked in reply.

"Shame on you! That's no way to treat your girlfriend," an old lady scolded. Yolo stifled a laugh and pretended to be hurt.

"She's not my...forget it!" he growled and marched off to the men's department.

He collected socks and drawers while she racked up on panties and bras. They would hit the mall later for clothing. The next stop was the hygiene aisle to get some toiletries. Then it was on to Big Shawn's apartment.

"Come on in," Bigs said opening the door and stepping aside so they could enter. The man inside stood up to be introduced.

"I'll just go..." Yolo mumbled and rushed into the showroom. She wasn't buying but wanted to fondle the weapons.

"Killa this is Ramel. Ra, Killa," Bigs introduced the two men to each other.

"Heard a lot about you," Ra said shaking the legend's hand.

"Can't believe everything you here," Killa said modestly, seeking to deflect the praise.

"Heard you wiped out a whole Jamaican posse at a funeral!" he said wide eyed like a child meeting his hero in person. Killa was a super hero to kids in New York City. They didn't play Batman, and fuck Spiderman. Everyone wanted to be Killa.

"Well…yeah, I did do that," he admitted as they sat.

Big Shawn sparked a blunt and passed some cold beer around. The conversation ranged from who was the best rapper to which singer had the fattest ass. Once that was settled, they got down to business. Bigs offered Ra ten grand on Killa's behalf to help with the hit. Ten grand he eagerly accepted.

"Our boy Fat is having a cookout at his crib. The whole crew will be there," Shawn relayed.

"One shot, one kill," Killa said happily. His smile dissipated instantly as Yolo returned and sat next to him.

"Like I told Bigs, I can get us in but I don't know about one shot. There will be like a hunned of them!" Ra added.

"Ever hear of Jim Jones?" Yolo tossed in tentatively.

"The rapper?" Ra scrunched his face. "They just be rapping, them dudes ain't killers!"

"Nah, not the rapper the imposter, the false prophet!" Killa corrected happily.

"Georgetown, Guyana," Bigs added as he caught on too.

Ra was too young to remember but old enough to Google. The room fell silent as he read up. A slow smile and nod formed as he caught up. "Don't drink the Kool-Aid!"

"Or…champagne," Yolo giggled and filled them in on her first hit. She put Treble and his whole crew down for dirt naps with one bottle of bubbly.

****

"You look nice, babe!" Yolo gushed when Killa came out of the bathroom dressed. He looked quite dapper in the linen suit and loafers.

"Stop...calling...me...babe!" he insisted once more.

"Ok babe," she said under her breath and giggled. "Wish I could come. I wanna kill too!"

"I'll bring you a plate and some champagne," he replied and cracked up.

"Ha ha, you can bring me some chicken...for the baby," she threw in and wiped the sarcastic smile off his face.

"Yeah," he remarked and left. Killa drove the rental car and met Ramel downtown. He got in and rode with him to Fat's large house in Henry County.

"You got that?" Killa asked Ra as he sped along the highway.

"That killa! It's in the glove box," he laughed.

"Nice!" he remarked as he carefully lifted out four ounces of fruity colored weed. "You should have saved some for us."

"Ta-dah!" Ra proclaimed and whipped out a neatly rolled blunt.

They couldn't smoke the pretty buds in the bag because they were poisoned. The world became a happier place with every toke of the potent plant. By the time they reached Fat's estate, they were both wearing goofy grins and cracking on each other.

"My wife would love that," Ra said pulling next to a convertible Audi.

"Give it to her then. He won't be driving it after today," Killa assured him. "None of them will."

"Hmm," Ramel hummed. All the men and women in attendance wore diamond, gold, and platinum and had thousands of dollars in cash on their persons.

"Fifty-fifty. To the victors goes the spoils," Killa said reading his mind.

The Black Mob associates and their women guests totaled just under a hundred people. Luckily, it wasn't catered because Killa didn't leave witnesses.

"Sup Ra," Oz greeted and gave Ramel a pound.

"Chillin', this my man…"

"Call me X," Killa interjected. He didn't want him to slip up and alert them to his presence.

"Where's Fat?" Ra asked and followed the directions into the den.

"My kind of cookout," Killa announced seeing a girl knelt before the fat man sucking his fat stubby dick.

"Want me to come back?" Ramel asked not wanting to interfere with his blowjob. That's just plain rude.

"Nah, you cool."

"This my man X. Just came down from up top. He gon' be working with me.

"Sup X?" Fat greeted in between loud breaths sounding like Darth Vader.

"Yo, I brought some killa weed," Killa said holding it up.

"Say lil' Lip, roll that up and pass it around," the host ordered.

"He's not going to make it," Killa laughed as Lip rolled blunt after blunt of weed. Handling it bare handed and licking cigars exposed him to the deadly cyanide mixed in.

Fat came with a grunt and held the woman in place, giving her no choice but to swallow. Once he finished he let her up wearing a bitter frown from the bitter semen.

"Give her one, she earned it," Fat laughed. The girl took a blunt and shot Killa a flirtatious glance as she passed.

"Yeah right," he laughed at her back.

One by one the blunts were passed around. Lip fell face first and died on the spot.

"You ain't smoking?" Ra offered holding out a blunt.

"Nah, I don't smoke," Fat replied.

"That's too bad," Killa remarked looking around the room for objects to beat him to death with. He settled on a set of golf clubs and handed Ra a driver.

"I'll go play clean up out there," Ra said of the few survivors around the backyard. "You got him?"

"Got him what?" Fat demanded and tried to heave himself out of the chair.

"This!" Killa said swinging the driver. "Fore!"

The golf club made a sickening crunch as it dented the fat man's forehead. The next blow split his wig and one of the next twenty blows killed the man. To add insult to injury, he took his phone and took several pictures of him.

"Turn left. Vogue. Work it girl," he teased the corpse.

Meanwhile Ramel went around the yard clubbing people with the club. Anyone with any sign of life or who didn't look dead enough got whacked upside the head. He then took the liberty of relieving them of stuff dead people have no use for. Fuck a dead man need a watch for? He don't. That's what. He also tracked down keys to the Audi.

Killa roamed around the house collecting cash and valuables. By the time Ra returned Killa had a pile of war booty in the blood splattered room. Ra came in and added to the spoils.

"You know what to do with that?" Killa dared pointing to ten neat bricks of coke.

"Do I!" he exclaimed and inspected them. "Five each."

"Nah, keep 'em. Let's split the cash and the rest is yours," Killa said showing his generosity. "Except this, I'll take this."

Ramel shrugged at the diamond encrusted pendant and chain. Dre was a little rough on jewelry anyway. Besides, the Audi meant some back shots were on the horizon.

"Preciate the help," Killa said when they finished loading the spoils in the cars.

"Anytime! I mean it, whenever you need me, just holla."

"I will, I'll leave the car with Bigs," he said. The men shared a pound and man hug before departing.

****

"Hey babe, I cooked," Yolo sang eagerly when Killa arrived. He just sighed heavily and shook his head.

"Here," he said handing Fat's phone with the pictures of his corpse.

"Cool!" Yolo cheered and flipped through them like a happy child.

"Figured you'd appreciate that, and this," he said tossing the jewels. The plan was to rock her to sleep and catch her off guard.

"Aw...my baby brought me a present," she said and scraped off a speck of dried blood.

She pulled up Big Rock's number from the contacts and sent pictures of the carnage. As expected, he called seconds later. Yolo put the phone on speaker so they could share the fun.

"I'm sorry, Fat is un-alive to take your call," she said trying her best to sound professional but failed and cracked up.

"Who is this? Yo, Yo, Yolo?" Rock managed.

"And Ki, Ki, Killa. And we're coming to see you soon. Real soon," she vowed.

Chapter 27

Killa was sleeping soundly after a night of multiple murders and mayhem. Even in his sleep, the man was sharp and alert. He had the feeling he was being watched and popped up to investigate.

"Really?" he asked seeing Yolo sitting Indian style watching him sleep. "How long have you been watching me?"

"About…four hours," she said confirming with the clock.

"You say that like it's not creepy," he said and rolled off the bed. He walked into the bathroom to relieve himself and felt it again. He turned and found Yolo standing in the doorway watching him pee. "Do you mind?"

"Not at all," she cheered staring at his dick.

Killa shook his head and finished doing his business. He gave it an extra shake since he had an audience.

"Ok, so who's next?" Killa asked watching Yolo scramble eggs.

"We could go over to Birmingham and kill Lil Redd. He's a real tough guy. I'm sure he took over for his daddy."

"My favorite," he said rubbing his hands together deviously. "They'll probably be waiting on us since it's so close?"

"We definitely need to go then!" she cheered then got sad. The corners of her lips turned down into a frown.

"Oh, what now?" Killa groaned. Yolo was definitely a lot of work. Between the hormones and being just plain crazy it was always something.

"I wanna kill some people too," she pouted, like a child denied a juice box. "The doctor said I have to do fun stuff so I can have a healthy baby."

"Ok, I'll let you kill Lil Redd n'dem," Killa said snickering at his southern slang.

"Thank you! Thank you! Thank you," Yolo clapped and danced in murderous joy.

After breakfast, the dangerous duo hopped on 20 east for the two-hour journey to Birmingham, Alabama. Yolo yapped the whole way. She was so excited to spend time with her crush.

"You sure the time only goes back one hour?" Yolo asked scrunching her face up. "Looks more like 20 years!"

Killa just shook his head and kept driving. What was there to say anyway, she was right. Passing through the historic downtown was indeed traveling back through time.

"We can stay at any hotel. They should be waiting on us," Yolo guessed correctly. Lil Redd was a very dangerous little man and look forward to the coming storm of violence.

"Don't worry, Kisha will put us up," he advised and re-opened the verbal floodgates once more.

"Kisha? Who's Kisha? I know you better not have me around none of your old girlfriends! You got some nerve…" she ranted on and on. Killa stifled a laugh and let her complain.

Yolo

"Killa!" A beautiful bubbly jet-black woman cheered when he turned into the driveway. Her large breasts bounced with her as she bounced with excitement. Yolo looked down at her own breasts jealously. Even filled out from pregnancy they didn't bounce. She made up her mind to kill the woman first chance she got.

"Hey Kish...ugh!" Killa grunted when the woman snatched him into a bear hug. His feet lifted off the ground from the embrace.

"And who is this pretty lil thing?" Kisha gushed and put Killa back down. She made her way around the car to squeeze her too. Yolo reached into her purse for a gun until Killa spoke and saved the woman's life.

"My um...girlfriend," he said barely able to get it out. It left a bad taste in his mouth that made him spit.

"Hey, there lil' mama! I see you finna have a baby!" she said hugging Yolo's neck.

"Finna!" Yolo replied since it was the only southern term she knew.

"Come on in, let me feed y'all," Kisha demanded and drug Yolo towards the small house.

"So...how do you guys know each other?" Yolo asked while Killa removed a bag from the trunk.

"He was close with my ol' man till he got kilt. He been looking out for me and the chillen err since," she said revealing Killa's soft side.

Yolo frowned in confusion at the contradiction. She was a murderer and had no soft side, no chill, no compassion, reason, or understanding. Then her baby kicked inside her.

****

"Ok, so which one of y'all bitch made niggas said my daddy should have left someone else in charge? Like he knew he was finna get blowed up," Lil Redd demanded as he addressed the Mob associates.

The man inherited the moniker Redd from his daddy. The 'Lil' part was because he was a lil' mutherfucker. But he had a big gun, a hair trigger, and a short temper. Good thing for Birmingham that Killa n'dem was here to see him.

"Alls I said was it may have been better to have someone older in charge. Someone used to doing thangs the old way," Penny replied calmly. He shot a glance around the room to see who snitched on him to the hot head.

"You miss my daddy don't you? That's what this about. Y'all growed up together, came up together, and you miss him," Lil Redd said trying to be understanding.

"I shole do! I..." Penny said, well tried to say, until Lil Redd fired a bullet into his forehead. That shut him up.

"Tell my daddy I said hey!" Lil Redd told the corpse. "Anybody else miss my daddy?"

"Hell nah, Un uh, Fuck yo' daddy," came the replies.

They all declared their allegiance to Lil Redd and the Black Mob. And they were all going to die for it.

"Good, cuz this crazy ass Yolo done wiped out the whole Atlanta mob. We closest so don't be surprised if she come here next!"

"Wish she would brang her ass down here with five million on her head. Brang that so called Killa too, make it a cool ten mil," Theo proclaimed.

This was going to be a classic example of the old adage, be careful what you wish for. Yolo was there and she did brang Killa with her.

****

"I'm all set, Baby. Ready when you are," Yolo said into her Bluetooth. She was perched comfortably on a rooftop across from the pool hall that served as Black Mob headquarters in Birmingham.

"Stop calling me baby," he demanded once more. "Get ready, I'm about to flush them out."

"K, Babe," she snickered and peered through the night vision sight attached to a high-powered rifle.

Killa used Fat's phone and called Lil Redd. The distinctive ring tone assigned to Mob members alerted Redd to take the call. He did a double take seeing Fat's name and number. He was pretty sure they didn't have cell towers in hell. The reception must suck down there.

"Fat?" Lil Redd asked tentatively upon taking the call.

"Uh no, Fat's dead. I killed him just like I'm going to kill you," Killa explained. "Now you can either burn or get shot. Your choice."

"I…" Redd said realizing the line was dead. He didn't know it yet, but he was too.

"What's the matter?" Theo asked seeing 100% Grade A fear on the man's face.

"Killa's here. He said we can burn or get shot. What does that mean?" he asked.

The question was to Theo but it was Killa who replied when a firebomb broke through the back window. Roland was too close and went up in flames. Before they had time to process what happened, another window broke and in came another cocktail.

"Let's get out of her!" Redd shouted needlessly as everyone ran for the front door. Roland led the way, it was only right, since he was on fire.

"Oh cool!" Yolo proclaimed as the flaming man came out. She allowed him a few steps before dropping him with a headshot. Theo hurdled the man on fire and Yolo gunned him down in mid-air.

"They shooting!" Lil Redd shouted and bust a left. He made it three whole feet before getting shot too. One by one, and two by two, Yolo shot down every member of the Black Mob in Birmingham.

"Have fun?" Killa asked as Yolo got into the car.

"I did! I did!" she shouted and kissed his cheek.

"Get off me," he said pushing her gently back into her own seat. "Who's next to die?"

"Um…wanna go to Cali? I love LA!"

Chapter 28

Yolo rambled on, like only Yolo could, as she and Killa made their way through the airport. Once they boarded she scooped her arm in his and laid her head on his shoulder. He just shook his head and held his tongue.

"So…you wanna join the mile high club?" Yolo suggested seductively once they were airborne.

"No!" Killa barked not even looking up from the movie playing on his phone. "Besides, I been a member for years."

"Guess we better wait until after I deliver our…baby. I'm gonna ride you like the Pony Express!" she vowed. "I'm gonna be like oh Killa! Yeah Killa! Fuck me, Killa! Fuck me! Fu…"

"Shut up," he said covering her mouth with his hand. Mothers covered their children's ears to shut off the X-rated outburst. A smiling flight attendant rushed over to investigate.

"Is everything ok?" she asked using an 'Are you crazy' tone.

"No, everything is not ok!" Yolo pouted and then stood. "My boyfriend knocked me up and now won't have sex with me!"

"Will you sit down?" Killa growled, pulling her back into her seat. "Cut it out!"

"Not until you promise to give me some. Promise!" she dared.

"Ok, ok, I'll fuck you. After you give birth you can get it," he lied. The only thing he planned to give her was a beautiful death.

"Ok babe," Yolo giggled then frowned from a sudden pain. "Uh oh."

"Uh oh what? Please don't uh oh," Killa pleaded watching her cradle her stomach. It was a waste of breath because once labor starts it doesn't stop. "It's too soon."

"Tell that to your baby," she replied with beads of sweat popping out of her forehead.

"We'll be landing shortly. An ambulance will be waiting," the flight attendant assured her.

As promised, an ambulance met the plane on the tarmac when they touched down at LAX. Yolo was placed on a stretcher and loaded on board.

"You're not coming?" Yolo asked as if she wanted to cry when Killa didn't get in with her.

"I gotta meet my people. I'll be there in a few," he assured her and turned to the driver. "Which hospital is she going to?"

"Cedar Sinai," he replied and closed the door.

Killa went through the airport to meet his close friend who was there to pick him up. Just like last time, Big Cyke was standing with the limo drivers holding up a sign bearing his name.

"My main man Killa," Cyke shouted. Killa stopped and broke into his best Crip walk. It might have been his best but it still sucked. "Please stop."

"You no like?" Killa asked as if wounded.

Yolo

"Stick to what you do best," the big homie advised.

"That's why I'm here. Gonna paint the town blue," he said referring to the head of the LA Black Mob.

"Azul you mean," Cyke laughed and explained.

Blue Johnson was born and raised in Compton, California. His gang related father named him after his bandana. He got his weight up the old-fashioned way by slinging crack and busting his gun. His hustle and violence attracted the Mob and he was put in charge of LA operations.

Being the man meant he no longer had to hide his sexuality. As a result, he changed his name from Blue to Azul. It actually meant the same thing but sounded gay. That's exactly what he was but Cyke thought it would be funny to leave that part out.

"Anyway, you can catch him in his club any night of the week," Cyke advised.

"Which club?" Killa wondered as they got seated in the low rider.

"Rough riders," Cyke said trying not to laugh.

"What, they ride bikes or something?"

"They ride something," he cracked up. "Anyway, where to?"

"Cedar Sinai. I'm having a baby," Killa admitted for the first time.

****

227

"Just relax and breathe," the delivery nurse said soothingly.

"Relax? Bitch, I got a whole person trying to come out of my vagina! How the fuck I'm 'posed to relax?" Yolo shot back. She glanced around the room for something to kill her with, but luckily nothing was in reach.

"You're three months early...something is weird with this heartbeat," the doctor announced as he checked on the baby. Yolo memorized his full name. She was going to do something weird to him if anything happened to her child.

"You sure you know what you're doing? Last time I gave someone an epidural she felt it when I cut off her foot," Yolo asked as the nurse performed that procedure.

All movement in the room paused to process the statement. In the end, they shrugged it off as labor pains.

"Just rel...uh...I um..." the doctor stammered as he prepared to go in and get the premature baby.

"Can we wait for my boyfriend?" Yolo whined causing the nurse to snicker. Quite a few mothers made that request when they arrived and most ended up giving birth alone and raising their child alone.

"If I had a dollar for every time I heard that, I'd..."

"Be a dollar short today!" Killa said as he walked into the room.

"Hey, there little fellow," the doctor said happily as he pulled a tiny baby boy from Yolo. He was small and underweight, but healthy. "He'll have to go into an incubator to cook for a couple of months."

"Cook! No one's cooking my baby!" Yolo shouted trying to sit up.

"Relax, it's a figure of...Doctor, you missed one," the nurse said urgently.

"One what?" both Mom and Dad shouted together.

Neither got an answer because the doctor was too busy pulling their daughter into the world.

"Oh my," Killa said and sank into a chair.

"A boy and a girl!" the nurse announced with glee. "Have you given any thought to names?"

"You do it," Yolo said in exhaustion.

Killa got up and went over to look at the paternal twins. Even though the babies were premature, they still had classic Forrest features.

"Sun...and Shyne," he announced looking from his son to his daughter.

"Sun and Shyne...I love it," Yolo repeated and fell asleep.

****

Killa was a jumbled up ball of mixed emotions as he stepped out of the hospital. He really wanted to go sit in private and sort things out, but Big Cyke was waiting in the parking lot. It went from bad to worse when the satellite phone began to ring.

It was Grandma's Biggie Smalls ring tone but he knew it was wifey. He got in the car and took the call in order to explain to both of them at the same time.

"So…what's up?" Sincerity asked. She closed her eyes real tight to listen for background noises. Sincerity was none too pleased with him traipsing around the country with any woman; especially Yolo.

"Over at Cedar Sinai with the homie Big Cyke fool," Killa joked in a mock LA accent.

"What happened? Is he ok?" she shot back full of concern.

"He's cool; I um…had to bring Yolo to have the babies…"

"I'm sorry, say that again!" Sincerity demanded.

"She had the babies," he blurted.

"Babies? That's plural; you said bies, what bies? Tell me this chick did not have twins! Killa, she better not have twins!"

"Um…" Killa replied cracking Cyke up.

He was so happy to see someone else get chewed out he pumped his fist. Meanwhile, Killa braced himself for a verbal smack but it never came.

"I see," she said with an eerie calm that unnerved Killa. "A bit early aren't we?"

"Yeah a few months premature. They have to stay in neonatal for 60 days," he replied.

"60 days? Ok, see you then," Sincerity said and clicked off the line.

"You good?" Cyke asked through his glee.

"Yeah…no. She's too calm, that's not good at all."

****

Killa dressed for the club in a rented suit. He wasn't quite sure of the dress code for the rough rider club so he opted for slacks and a button down shirt. You can't go wrong with slacks and loafers. He tucked a borrowed pistol into the small of his back and got into a borrowed Benz. He followed the turn-by-turn directions of the navigation system until he arrived at the club. He realized instantly what Cyke had been laughing at.

"Fuckin' Cyke! I got you for this!" he said when his friend took the call. A six-foot drag queen in 6-inch heels winked and waved as it passed the car.

"Me? What I do!" Cyke asked and cracked up again.

"Shit ain't funny yo. Dennis Rodman just blew me a kiss," he shot back.

Killa hung up, took a deep breath, and headed into the gay bar. A gay funk punched him in the nose as soon as he stepped inside. It smelled like ass grease, sweat, and perfume.

"You sure you in the right place?" the only woman in the place asked seeing his expression.

Only straight men reacted like that upon entering. The large woman was the bouncer.

"Yeah...um, yes," Killa barked then softened trying to sound gay. It didn't work.

"Yeah, ok," the stud laughed.

She knew Azul often held business meetings here to keep people off balance. Most dudes agreed to his terms just to get the hell out of there.

"He's in the VIP. You can't miss him."

"Can't miss him," Killa repeated as he walked towards VIP. It was a relatively short distance but he still had to dodge a cowboy, an Indian, and Tinkerbell.

He wondered what the stud meant by 'can't miss him' and just knew it wasn't good. He was right. When he saw Azul, he stopped dead in his tracks and shook his head. How could anyone miss the tall man, in the blue dress, wearing a blue wig, blue pumps, and twerkin'?

Killa imagined himself pulling his gun and shooting him dead on the spot. He quickly shook his head to erase the foolish plan like an Etch-a-Sketch. These homos would beat him to death before he made it to the door. Probably scratch his eyes out.

"Might just let this one live," Killa thought aloud.

At that moment, he just wanted to get as far away from the freaks as possible. Instead, he let out a deep sigh and joined the spectators tossing money at the dance.

Azul didn't need the money, but did crave the attention. He hid his inner bitch for so long that now he flaunted it. Being the pipeline between good Mexican drugs meant everyone just had to accept it. Azul was working it too. He whipped his hair from side to side and shook his ass.

There was a slight wardrobe malfunction when he tried to drop it like it's hot. He dropped a little too fast and one of his balls got loose. He tucked it away, and kept right on twerking. He did a double take when he noticed the new face in the crowd. As soon as the song ended, he rushed over to Killa to investigate.

Yolo

"Hey handsome," Azul said flirtatiously. The greeting was actually a question of who and why.

"Sup," Killa greeted.

The sight of the blue bra strap under the blue dress irked him. The man had on a blue thong too but Killa wouldn't see it. The coroner would be taking it off his corpse first thing in the morning.

"Oh you're straight!" the sissy said waving a finger like being straight was naughty. Gay men are still men and love virgins. It's a badge of honor for them to turn a new man. Sorta like vampires except they suck dicks not blood.

Azul used his position of power to his gay advantage. He often seduced men in exchange for business. If you wanted to break bread, you had to break bread.

"I um…forget it," Killa said and gave up.

He would just have to catch him another time. Maybe snipe him at the next gay day parade. There were too many witnesses to murder him here, and he couldn't take the falsetto voice another second.

"Wait, where you going?" Azul pouted and grabbed Killa's hand.

"Back to my hotel," he admitted.

"I'm coming too!" Azul insisted.

He hooked his arm under Killa's and waved bye-bye to his crew. Killa looked like he wanted to cry as he walked arm in arm from the club with a man. A man taller than he was.

"Want some head while we drive?" Azul offered generously.

Sa'id Salaam

"I would but I didn't bring my DC 2000," Killa replied.

"Huh?" he asked unfamiliar with the deadly device.

"Nothing. I can't drive while getting head," he admitted. Every time he got head while driving, he ended up swerving like a DUI.

"Pull over there!" Azul said licking his lips. He pulled a pair of blue rhinestone kneepads from his blue purse.

Killa whipped across all lanes of traffic and came to a screeching halt on the shoulder. Azul was so happy he clapped and danced in the seat.

"I see someone can't wait to put something in someone's mouth," the sissy cheered.

"You have no idea," Killa replied. Azul pulled the kneepads on and got out as Killa got out and came around.

"Close your eyes and say ah," Killa instructed.

Azul dropped to his knees and complied. "Ahhhh," he said stifling a smile upon hearing the zipper unzipped. He felt something hard enter his mouth and realized it was too hard.

Gun barrel hard.

Killa shoved the pistol down to the man's tonsils. When he heard the gag, he tugged on the trigger. The hollow point slug flattened as it entered his forehead. It passed through his confused brain and knocked his wig off as it came out the back. Azul sat there for a second with his mouth and eyes wide open. Finally, gravity caught up with him and pulled him over.

"That was fun," Killa giggled as he pulled away from the murder scene. Murder always made him horny and that night was no different. He shook off the thought of hitting a club and pulled out his phone.

"Hello?" Daphine barked into her phone as she took the call from the unknown number.

The poor girl had slept with so many strange men from the club it took five minutes before she remembered who he was. Once she recalled the one night stand, she eagerly accepted the invitation for another one. Killa gave her the name of his hotel and his room number. She arrived just as he stepped from the shower.

"Mph!" Daphine grunted as Killa opened the door butt naked. She was dressed to kill with all of her etceteras. That wouldn't do at all.

"Go take all that stuff off! All of it," he ordered pointing towards the bathroom.

Daphine giggled and complied. She went in and removed her weave, lashes, contacts, push up bra, and butt pads. A few minutes later, she emerged looking like Side Show Bob.

Once again, Killa fucked Side Show Bob, twice.

Chapter 29

"Wow," Yolo whispered as she looked down at her sleeping infants in the incubator. "Sun and Shyne...my babies."

It suddenly hit her like a ton of bricks that killing children was wrong. Dead wrong. A single tear managed to get by and ran down her cheek. She realized at that moment why Killa wanted to kill her.

"Unless I kill you first."

"Kill who?" Killa asked as he came up behind her. It's true that bad boys move in silence and violence.

"Nobody," she said twisting up her lips ruefully. "Sup with our boy Blue?"

"At the morgue turning blue," Killa retorted. "Who's next?"

"Let's see...we can go down to San Diego and fire The Captain or shoot up to the bay and shoot up Cheese," she replied after pausing to recall who would have taken over when Rock killed the bosses. She remembered giving quite a few promotions herself after cutting off the local bosses. "You think maybe we should split up?"

"Nah, we're better together," he shot back without having to think about it.

"Okay," Yolo sang and giggled despite her confusion. Did he want her close so they could be together or so he could kill her? "I can be released in the morning. Can we visit SeaWorld?"

"...I guess," Killa replied with a curious frown.

The more time he spent around her the more he realized she was human after all. A confused little girl guided in the wrong direction. A slow smile spread on his face as a murderous thought came to mind.

"What?" Yolo smiled deviously to match his. She recognized the violence just below the mirth.

"Do they let you feed the sharks at SeaWorld?"

****

"Good for that cocksucker! And I mean literally!" Cheese barked into the phone as he viewed the pictures of Azul stretched out on a slab.

"Good for him, but bad for me!" Rock yelled in reply. "That faggot was the connect between us and Mexico. The Chinese find out about this and we lose them too!"

"Well, if they come up to San Fran I'm personally dropping them off the dock of the bay! Wish they would!"

"Funny, that's the same thing Lil Redd said. Now he's dead! Him and the whole gang, dead! Do not underestimate these two..."

Cheese sat the phone down and pulled Ne-Ne's thong off. She giggled like the teen she was when he began playing between her legs. Her and other young girls were his weakness. Every soldier has a chink in their armor and pubescent girls were his.

Likewise, the so-called Captain down in San Diego had a frailty of his own. The fat bastard would not stop eating. The man spent half the day sleeping and the other half eating. He really was a Captain and spent most of his time on his boat.

A coin flip granted The Captain a few more days to wallow in his gluttony. Big Cyke provided another car and more guns for the drive north. Yolo wasn't back to 100% after childbirth, but half a Yolo was better than no Yolo.

Killa watched her out of the side of his eye as she worked over a large ice pop. She saw him peeping as he drove and began to really put on.

"Mm, this is so good!" she exclaimed running her tongue up and down the shaft.

Killa turned his head in her direction and watched her inch it down her throat until she gagged. He got so hard, so fast, that his vision blurred.

"Watch out!" Yolo shrieked as Killa nearly missed a semi truck.

"Then cut it out 'for you kill us both!" he yelled. He made the rest of the drive with an erection straining against his pants. No wonder they made it in record time.

"Where we headed?" Yolo asked as Killa whipped through Oakland like he knew where he was going. That was because he did.

"Gonna link up with my nigga Z-Ro. He'll know how we can get next to this Cheese dude."

Sa'id Salaam

"Then we gon' cut the Cheese! Get it? Cut the Cheese?" Yolo said cracking herself up.

Killa didn't find it funny but was amused by her. It started with a smile on the corner of his mouth but ended up with him laughing along with her.

They just had a moment.

****

"Hell yeah, I know that nigga!" Z-Ro snarled.

The killers could tell immediately that he harbored some malice towards the man himself. They needed to know if it was personal or business. It made a difference. Business beef usually stems from hatred and jealousy. Personal beef is stronger, deadlier even. Z-Ro went on and explained why it was the latter.

"The fuck ass old man preys on these young girls. He got my little sister pregnant. She was only 15 but wanted to keep it. When she refused to get an abortion he choked her and dumped her body in an alley!"

"Which alley?" Killa asked intending to return the favor.

"You won't be able to get close to him without a vagina. That's why I haven't murked him myself," Z-Ro relayed.

"I have a vagina!" Yolo volunteered with her hand up.

"You may be too old," he said trying to gauge her age. "He likes them young!"

"I ain't but 15," Yolo said pouting, ducking, and looking every bit of 15 years old.

240

Both Killa and Z-Ro nodded in agreement. She was their way in.

"I think I'll have some fun with ol' Cheese before I kill him," Yolo said as she and Killa entered the local mall. She pointed at some butterfly knives in a window.

"No. Just get in, shoot him in his head, and get out!" Killa barked. "You just gave birth and this dude chokes chicks!"

"Oh ok," Yolo pouted like a truculent child. "Can I still get my knives anyway?"

"Get 'em, but you're using a gun. Ya heard?" he insisted again.

"Yes daddy, oops...I mean baby daddy," she giggled and skipped off into the knife store.

Once Yolo stocked up on knives, throwing stars, and his and hers brass knuckles, they set out to do some shopping. Walking through the busy mall, they were able to figure out what girls in Cheese's age range liked to wear. They followed a group of giggling teens into a store and bought what they bought.

"That's him right there!" Killa said as they left the store.

They spotted the child molester luring a young girl away from the game room. If not for the bodyguards and crowd, they would have ended this chapter right here. Instead, they could only watch helplessly as the child was led away.

Killa and Yolo were both in a somber mood for the rest of the day. They ate take out in their hotel room in virtual silence. Even though they climbed into the same bed, they slept separately. Once again, Killa awoke to find Yolo staring down at him.

"Ugh! Would you stop that shit!" he grumbled and rolled out of bed.

"Stop what?" Yolo giggled and followed him to the bathroom. She wanted to watch him pee again but he closed the door in her face. "Meanie," she said and stuck her tongue out at him through the door. She heard him enter the shower so she stepped out to find breakfast.

"Mm hm," Killa said sarcastically when he came out and saw breakfast.

"You're welcome, Babe," she smiled understanding the unspoken thanks. She switched places with him and entered the shower.

"Here," Killa said displaying a small .40 caliber pistol. He tucked it into the kiddie backpack that was a part of her costume.

"Thanks," she replied with a smirk.

Killa didn't know her quirks well enough to know it was her smile of defiance. She dropped the towel from around her to change the subject.

"I um…" Killa frowned as her naked body stole his train of though. Besides a slight pouch in the middle, the girl was fine. Killa mumbled incoherently and stepped outside to call his family.

****

"I hope we don't have to be here all day," Killa said as they entered the game room.

"I do!" Yolo shouted and ran inside. She whipped her head from side to side trying to decide what to play first. She hopped and clapped when deciding upon a vintage Ms. Pac-man game.

"Kids," Killa chuckled and went to shoot zombies. Killa got his wish when Cheese slithered in a few minutes later.

The large bodyguard with him wore a perturbed look on his face. The pay was great but he wasn't with the pedophile part. He should have quit because he was about to die because of it.

"That's a new one there ain't it?" Cheese asked licking his chops at Yolo. The pigtails and bobbie socks made her look ten years younger and that was right up the sick fuck's alley.

"Nah, boss," the hired gun replied dryly. Dry or not, he was about to get wet for being a sellout. The words were barely out of his mouth before the boss moved on the child.

"You're pretty good!" Cheese said in a soft voice reserved for children. That was how he spoke to them before molesting them. After that, he put them on the track and it was 'Bitch better have my money.'

"Thanks, Mister," she replied over her shoulder without looking back.

"You must have one of these games at home. Would you like the new system?" he offered as bait.

"Ain't got no home," she said.

"No? So where yo' mama?" he asked feeling the blood rush down below.

"I'on know? I stay in a group home."

"Let's go!" he demanded, practically snatching her away from the machine. The group home girls were the easiest. A meal, pair of colorful sneakers, and the rest is smooth pimping.

Yolo and Killa made eye contact as she rushed by. Killa waited a second and discreetly followed them out to the parking lot. He could afford to lag since he knew where they were going.

"Here you go lil' mama," Cheese said stealing a grab on Yolo's ass as he helped her into the car.

"Stop!" she said spinning and swatting his hand away so he wouldn't feel her pad. He was going to need a pad himself for what she had planned.

"Fucking hard head!" Killa fumed when he realized Yolo ditched the gun and took the knives. "We got people to kill all over the country and you playing!"

"We straight!" Cheese barked when they reached the apartment that he used to deflower young girls.

"Call when you need me," the help said as they got out. He waited until he got all the way in before pulling away. He didn't get far though.

"Excuse me, a little help?" Killa called out waving his hands. If he hadn't been standing in the path, the man would have kept right on driving.

"What?" he barked as Killa approached the descending window.

"Just wanted to let you know you had a hole in your head."

"A hole in my what?" he shot back and got shot.

"Your head," Killa giggled and walked away.

"Take your clothes off, all of them. Socks. Panties, everything," Cheese ordered once they got inside.

Yolo smiled as she pulled off her backpack and pulled out her weapons of mass destruction. She popped in her fangs and raised the knives.

"I'm ready," Yolo sang causing Cheese to look up from his undressing. All he had on was socks and an erection, that's a fucked up way to die.

"Fuck you got going on?" he asked as if it were some kind of game. He got the point when she stuck the point of one of the knives into his beer belly. "Bitch!"

"Your mama," she giggled and ducked a blow. Every time he swung at her she dipped, ducked, and stuck him.

Blood covered the room from floor to ceiling as the battle raged on. Cheese was losing blood and steam but so was Yolo. The tough girl underestimated the effect of giving birth and was exhausted. Her foot slipped in a blood puddle and Cheese was able to catch her.

"Now you die bitch!" he screamed as he lifted her by her throat. Her wind was cut off instantly from the pressure. In a panic, she dropped the knives and tried to peel the death grip from her neck.

Yolo kicked and clawed but to no avail. Cheese understood his wounds were fatal and planned to take her with him. Her hearing dimmed followed by her vision. Everything began to fade and she knew she was dying. Her babies popped in her mind as her life flashed before her. Somewhere in the distance, a gun fired. She wasn't sure what it had to do with until Cheese released his death grip. Down they went with him landing on top.

"Fucking hard headed!" Killa grumbled as he kicked the dead man off Yolo. He tossed her over his shoulder and whisked her away.

Yolo awoke on the drive back to the motel but kept her eyes closed. She strained to comprehend why he saved her. She was dead. Cheese had killed her, so why did he save her?

Chapter 30

"Still not talking to me?" Yolo asked with her lip poked out. They were halfway back to LA and he still hadn't said a word. Even now, he just sucked his teeth without turning his attention from the highway. "I'll take that as a no."

"Take it as a hell no!" he corrected. "Call this Captain dude; let him know we're on the way.

"Ok!" she said happily and made the call from Fat's phone. By now, Fat's phone was the equivalent to the kiss of death. Killa and Yolo on the phone was like having the Grim Reaper at your front door.

"It's them," Captain whispered when he saw the name on the phone. He dropped it and scurried away so they couldn't come through the line and get him. His woman just shook her head at the display.

"It went to voicemail," Yolo said sounding disappointed.

"So, leave a message," he said like it should have been the obvious thing to do.

"Hey, it's me, Yolo…"

"And Killa!" Killa leaned in and added.

"And Killa; and we're coming to kill you guys. All of you; ok, bye!" she sang waving like he could see her.

The two killers had a good laugh once she hung up. The mood in the car lightened allowing for small talk.

"I've been meaning to ask you...did you really kill 100 people before you turned 21?" Yolo asked sounding star struck.

"Nah, that's a myth. An urban legend," he admitted breaking her heart. "Actually, I was 22."

Yolo cheered, clapped, and then went suddenly somber. Killa was about to ask her what was wrong until he saw for himself. The sign for Cedar Sinai passed overhead reminding them both of what was there.

"I gotta stop in LA and holla at the big homie. He claims he got something for me," Killa offered.

"Cool, I can see my babies while we're there," she said.

He put the blinkers on and merged over for the unscheduled trip. The captain would just have to wait a few more hours to get murdered.

****

"Aw..." Yolo cried when she looked in and saw the twins holding hands in the incubator.

"Cool," Killa admitted since he was too cool to saw 'aw.'

After an hour of gawking, Killa led Yolo away. Thirty minutes later, they met up with Big Cyke.

"No...fucking...way!" Yolo exclaimed in stunned disbelief when Cyke demonstrated their new toy.

"Easy too," Killa added as he took over the controls to the deadly device. "I'll take it! How much?"

Yolo

"On the house. It's a gift from the homies down in San Diego. With the Mob gone they can eat again," Cyke replied. That seemed to be the sentiment all over the country.

"Can I do it?" Yolo asked bouncing like a 5 year old. Killa twisted his lips to keep from laughing and let her take over the controls.

"Damn, she rocking that shit better than you! Better than me!" the big homie exclaimed.

"Yeah, yeah. I guess I'll let her do the honors then," Killa admitted. He turned to his longtime friend and exchanged a pound and a hug. "Love you Cyke."

"Jihad," he corrected. "Love you too and remember, laa ilaha illallah!"

"True dat!" Killa nodded and agreed. Yolo twisted her pretty face to the strange words so he explained. "Nothing has the right to be worshipped except God, alone.

"True dat," she smiled and gave Jihad a pound. "I would hug you but my man be getting jealous."

"Get in the car!" he barked.

****

"So how long we gotta be out here?" Janice whined as the yacht pulled away from the dock. The woman bitched, moaned, and complained all day everyday but she had some good head, so it was cool.

249

"You can leave if you want! Swim your ass back to shore!" The Captain spat. It sounded hard but she heard his voice trembling in fear.

"I'm cool," she said wisely. "Want some head?"

"Fuck kind of question is that? Of course I want some head!" The Captain collapsed the deck chair so she could get to his dick under the big ass belly.

Janice worked the fat, stubby dick like a pro hoe. She spit, licked, sucked, and gnawed on it like a puppy with a chew toy. The blow had just gotten good when Captain noticed an unidentified flying object. No, not E.T., but a drone.

The once innocuous hobby craft was retrofitted with a camera and two fully automatic Mac 10s. Each machine pistol held a two hundred and fifty round drum of ammo meaning it could really fuck some shit up.

"That's called 'the flute,'" Yolo said in reference to the technique Janice was using. No sooner than she said it, she switched to the 'whistle while you work.' "She must have an app for that."

"Damn, I almost hate to interrupt," Killa said truthfully. "I wouldn't want to get killed while I'm getting head. Then again..."

"Remember what I gave you some head?" Yolo said trying to be sexy.

"No! Anyway, time to say good-bye to The Captain."

"What the fuck is that?" the captain asked as it drew closer.

For a reply, the small aircraft belched a flurry of .45 ACP rounds at them. Janice spit his dick out and stood. She tried to run but got gunned back down. The fat bastard rolled off the lounge chair a split second before Yolo shredded it with another burst of machine gun fire.

"Fat fucker is pretty fast," Yolo giggled as she chased the man around the deck.

"Damn it! Almost had him," Killa cheered by her side. Holes opened in the deck right on his heels. When the fat man ran out of deck, he leapt off the side. "Oh shit!"

"Ugh!" The Captain grunted as a slug hit him in his big ass before he hit the water.

Yolo circled the drone around for the kill. She was just about to hit the trigger until she had a better idea.

"Is that…" she asked with glee.

"It is! It is!" Killa cheered at the sight of an approaching dorsal fin. "Turn on the recorder!"

"I'm on it!" she shouted and hit record.

The shark seemed to smile at the massive meal. He would be forced to share as two more fins appeared. The carnivorous fish snatched chunks off the man filling the water with blood. That attracted more sharks and started a feeding frenzy.

"That was fun," Yolo giggled and brought the drone back.

"It was. Who's next?"

Chapter 31

"Err body talkin' 'bout heaven. Heaven, heaven, heaven, err body wanna go to heaven! But heaven ain't free! Ain't sh...uh, nothing free!" Pastor Roland Anderson said catching himself before he cursed, again. Last time he referred to the congregation as mutherfuckers. It took a month for them to get over it.

The good Reverend Roland had a foul mouth to go along with his foul manners. He wasn't much of a preacher either since he didn't believe in God. Church was a non-profit cash cow that hid his money laundering service. Black Mob dope boys ran dirty cash through him and it came back crispy clean.

He was once self-employed until Casper got wind of it. He sent the late, great Grimsley down to Mississippi with an offer he couldn't refuse. He certainly couldn't wear his fancy hats if he didn't have a head. Can't carry it in your hand because you're dead.

"Heaven got money! A whole lot more then y'all moth...than y'all put in the plate last week. How we 'posed to eat if ain't sh...eh, nothing on the plate? Now break bread damn it! Damn ain't a curse either. I seen it in the bible. I think," he preached.

"Not that much!" Yolo said a little too loudly for church. She grabbed Killa's wrists to stop him from dropping a thick roll of cash in the basket. He held it up for a second so the perfidious pastor could peep it.

"Why not? I'm going to take it back anyway. Over his dead body," Killa chuckled.

Yolo winked at the preacher and got his full attention. He turned it up a notch for the new meat. That was one of the perks of being a piss poor pastor. He hit all the women in the congregation at least once. Married, single, young, and old; he ran through them all.

"What did you do?" Killa wondered when he saw the change in the man's demeanor.

"Just put out a lil' bait and he bit," she giggled.

They only half listened as the man strutted like a rooster, whooping and hollering about nothing. He told so many lies about God Killa subconsciously cast a glance up to see if a bolt of lightning was coming. It didn't, but no matter, he was dying today anyway. And it was going to be brutal.

"Yes Lawd, I see some new pu...faces in the house. Y'all stand up and introduce y'all selves," he said looking directly at Yolo. She had just the right amount of cleavage to make Killa invisible.

"Introduce ya self," Yolo teased with an elbow to Killa's rib.

"Nah," he replied to her while raising a hand to wave. Yolo huffed and stood to do the honors.

"Hey y'all! I'm Yolonda and dis my brudda Ki, Ki, um Keith," Yolo said making it up as she went along. The pastor's smile broadened hearing the man next to her was her brudda. That's deep south for brother.

"Yes Lawd!" he repeated and went back to lying on God. He wrapped up with a prayer and class was dismissed.

"Wait for it. Wait…for it," Yolo giggled as they prepared to leave. The preacher was by their side before their first step hit the ground.

"Nice to meet you Rev, if y'all will excuse me," Killa begged off and left him alone with the bait.

"Hey Pastor," Yolo said ducking her head shyly.

"Hey ya' self sweet thing," he told her breasts. "Y'all just moved to town?"

"Un uh. We just passing through. We staying at the motor lodge for the night and gone in the mawnin," she said casting her pretty brown eyes up at him.

"You look like you in need of some spiritual healing," he suggested, as he looked her over.

"What if I'm in need of some dick?" she asked truthfully.

"That's what I meant," he assured her. "I'se here to help."

"So, want me to bend over this a here pew and let you do your bizness?" she offered.

The parasite pastor pondered for a second before answering.

"Too many people here now. Come back tonight so I can nail your ass to the cross!" he cheered triumphantly.

****

"Did he really say that?" Killa asked incredulously when Yolo returned to the car and filled him in. "Someone needs to nail his blasphemous ass to a cross!"

"Oh, stop in there," Yolo ordered pointing her finger.

"Here? Why?" he asked pulling into the hardware store parking lot.

"I need a hammer and nails," she replied wickedly. "So I can nail his ass to a cross."

"You're not going alone," he said firmly. "Look what happened last time. I had to come in and save your ass."

"That was a fluke. I got lightheaded, trust me; I'm fine. I got him, 'Sides you need to run around town and take care of the rest," she said in one breath. As much as she appreciated him saving her, she was embarrassed by it. Now she needed redemption, and Pastor was it.

"I guess," he conceded. He did want to move on to the next city and kill more people.

"This will work," she exclaimed picking up a pneumatic nail gun.

"So will this," he said grabbing an axe.

It was going to be a messy night. No, not timeline bitching and hating messy, but bone crunching and blood splattering messy. After paying for the killing apparatus, they retreated to the room to get some rest.

This time Killa insisted on double beds and got it. He was first to shower and climb into bed. A few minutes later Yolo came out in his t-shirt. She walked right past the empty bed and climbed in with him.

Yolo

"A-yo, do you mind" Killa complained.

"Not at all," she giggled and snuggled up close. Killa shook his head and closed his eyes.

The alarm of Killa's phone alerted them from their sleep. The clock read 9 pm. It was time to kill. Both killers rolled out of bed and got dressed. They grabbed the tools of their trade and hit the road. The plan was to drop her off back at the church while he went to murder the barber, the baker, and the candlestick maker. Yup, he was going to get it too. He came up with a way to move coke in the candles and was about to get snuffed out.

****

"Lawd, Lawd, Lawd!" Reverend Anderson moaned when Yolo sashayed into the church.

"Can you please stop saying that?" she winced. His constant taking of the Lord's name in vain hurt her soul.

"Ok?" he replied curiously. He didn't believe anyway, so it didn't matter to him. "What's in the bag?"

"This..." she said pulling out the nail gun. "...is a nail gun."

"Huh?" he asked and got a nail driven right into his forehead. "Ow!"

"Ow is right," Yolo laughed and put one in his knee. He realized things weren't going well and turned to run. That didn't go well either with a nail in his knee.

"W, w, wa, wait!" he pleaded holding up his hands and getting shot in them.

"N, n, n, no I w, w, won't wa, wa, wait," she taunted and put another nail in him. They weren't fatal, but they hurt badly. "Now get against the wall and put your hands up!"

"Yeow!" he screeched as he complied and got nailed to the wall. The large cross over the pulpit was too high so that would have to do.

Yolo ran nails through his pants and shirt as well as his palms. His screams reached the high heavens when she put a nail in his bunions. She nailed his feet to the floor right through his wing tips.

"Ok, ok, you win," he panted in defeat. "The money is in my office. The b, b, black satchel under my desk."

"Money?" Yolo inquired raising one eyebrow curiously.

"Yeah, tell Big Rock I'm sorry. It's all there, one million."

"I'll be right back," she said and went to check out his claim.

Sure enough, one million dollars in neat stacks were loaded in a bag. Yolo scooped it up and turned to leave. Something caught her eye on the way out bringing a smile to her face. She skipped happily over to the gas line and disconnected it.

"S, s, so w, we good?" Anderson asked hopefully when she came back with the bag.

"I am," she laughed and headed for the door. She walked out and hopped in his car and called Killa.

"I'm…a little…busy right…now," Killa said over the ear piercing screams. Getting chopped up with an axe while still alive is obviously painful.

"Ok, I was calling to let you know I got a ride. The preacher let me use his," she said before being cut off by the thunderous roar of the church exploding.

"What the hell was that?" he quizzed.

"The preacher. See you at the room."

****

"Honey you're home," Yolo sang as the door opened. In walked Killa covered in blood. The blood of three different men. "Oh my."

"Oh my is right," he muttered heading straight to the bathroom. Yolo jumped up and followed him.

"I got money," she smiled, and then smiled brightly when he peeled off the bloody shirt.

"Keep it," he blurted pulling off the pants and boxers at the same time.

"It's a lot!" she cheered watching his dick dangle when he moved. "A whole mil…"

"Keep it," he repeated and stepped inside the shower. He flinched from the burst of cold water then adjusted the temperature.

Yolo twisted her lips in thought trying to figure out why he would give her a million dollars. Was he going to kill her and take it back just like the money he put in the collection plate?

She shook the thought out of her head. She quickly stripped and stepped inside the shower behind him.

"What are you doing?" he barked when she pulled the washcloth away.

"Helping," she replied and began washing him. Blood swirled down the drain as she washed it away. "Turn!"

Killa was too tired to resist so he turned to face her. She thoroughly cleaned his head, face, and chest. She deliberately skipped his genitals and cleaned his legs and feet. She was simply saving the best for last.

Killa blew his breath as if frustrated when she grabbed his dick with the hot, soapy cloth. All that huffing and puffing but his ass ain't say stop. Instead, he grew rock hard in her hands.

He looked down at the pretty girl but she was too busy looking down at his dick. She dropped the washcloth and used her hands to stroke his thick shaft. It didn't take long before it pulsed and throbbed.

"Shit!" Killa grunted and exploded. He came so hard it hit her stomach with velocity. She kept right on stroking until he stopped skeeting.

"You're welcome," Yolo said and stepped out of the shower. She grabbed a towel and left closing the door behind her.

"Thank you," he said softly towards the door.

Chapter 32

For the next couple of weeks Yolo and Killa crisscrossed the country causing multiple murders and mayhem. They managed to keep the Black Mob completely off balance by bouncing coast-to-coast and state-to-state. No one knew where they might show up next.

From Bangor, Maine down to Eatonville, Florida where the notorious Pista Pete was held up. The Miami gunrunner figured he could duck off into the smaller town until the storm passed. Figured wrong because hurricane Yolo switched directions and blew his house down. Literally.

"I'll huff, and I'll puff, and I'll...what comes next?" she paused to ask.

"Blow your house down," Killa helped out.

"Yeah, yeah, that's it! I'll blow your house down," she said then paused to giggle before pulling the trigger. The grenade launcher did what grenade launchers do and launched a grenade. The explosive went straight through the front door and blew the house down.

Pista Pete came flying out the window and Killa gunned him down out of the air like he was skeet shooting.

"Next!" Yolo shouted like you know who and it was off to Anchorage, Alaska. They were both disappointed not to see any igloos or Eskimo. The big city looked just like any other big city. It also had a booming drug trade, which meant Black

Mob. Yolo had Killa, which meant no more Black Mob. A couple of well-placed car bombs wiped out the faction in one long night.

Next, they brought the pain to Portland, Maine. Next, they made the Windy City look shitty, and made a big mess in Texas, New York, Philly, Oklahoma, Vegas, and Tahoe.

"I wonder how they are…Sun and Shyne," Yolo pouted like a mother missing her babies.

"We're about to find out. I heard we missed one in LA," Killa lied. Truth be told, he wanted to see the twins as well.

"Thank you! Thank you! Thank you," Yolo cheered and clapped like a schoolgirl. She babbled the whole way back to LA.

When they arrived at Cedar Sinai, he let Yolo go ahead so he could talk to the doctor. She approached the window like she was afraid. Her fears dissipated the moment she saw them.

"Look at how much you guys have grown!" she exclaimed. The twins opened their eyes and looked up at her. "My babies."

"Two more weeks," Killa advised when he returned. The babies turned to look up at him then back to their mom. Mixed emotions swept through his being as he looked at his children. A month ago, he wanted nothing more than murder; now, he wasn't sure.

"I guess we better step it up then huh?" she replied.

Step it up they did. Phoenix, Boston, and Bismarck. Richmond, Raleigh, Nashville, and finally New Orleans.

"The big sleazy," Killa said changing the name on the sign as he read it.

"You gotta say Nawlins," Yolo corrected. "Home of Lil Man."

"So where this nigga be at? Let's knock his block off so we can move to the main event," he stated meaning Big Rock. Only days remained. It was time to end this.

"First, he is a she and you can't get anywhere next to her with a dick. Especially a pretty dick like yours," she giggled.

"Ok, first of all...stop playing with my dick while I'm asleep," he chided.

"Huh?" she giggled again and then got down to business explaining the Black Mob operations in The Big Easy.

The late Daddy Mack and cousin Lil Man were big time studs. They cornered the pussy market then moved on to heroin. Using their bevy of beauties to set up rivals they easily took over the drug trade. They made a female only strip club their base of operation meaning a dude couldn't even get close.

"The Pink Palace has a no penis policy. And you sir, have a penis," Yolo stated. "I'm gonna need a party dress."

Killa pulled over to a chic boutique and let her out. He took the opportunity to call his family.

"Mm hm," Sincerity hummed upon answering the phone. Killa smiled at the picture of her with arms crossed and her lip poking out.

"I know babe. Anyway, how are you? The kids, Grandma, and Cameisha?"

"Err body fine. When you coming down?" she pouted. Killa comforted her as best he could. Yolo came back just in time to hear him say 'it'll all be over in a few days.'

She slid silently back into the car and pondered on what he meant. What would be over, her? Was he still planning to kill her? He had been so nice lately. They ate, slept, and killed together just like a real couple. Still...she did kill his kid.

Chapter 33

The killer couple hid in plain sight and checked into a fancy French quarter hotel. Killa shook his head when Yolo ordered a room with a king-sized bed. One bed, which meant them sleeping together once again.

He would never admit it, but he had actually gotten used to waking up with the lunatic cuddled up next to him. Even if she did pull his dick out in his sleep. There was no sex even though Yolo made a big production when her six weeks past, and was shot down.

Yolo was in her feelings about getting turned down. Men had been trying to fuck her since she was a child. But the only man she ever loved, the father of her children, refused to touch her.

"You straight? Need…anything?" Yolo asked, offering herself to him once again, once they reached their room. She was hoping he would say yes, and make mad passionate love to her. Or at least fuck her, but no such luck.

"Nah, I'm cool," he replied and rolled over. A few seconds later, he was sleeping soundly and snoring loudly from the long drive.

"I'm not," Yolo said with her lip poked out. She laid down next to him and pouted herself to sleep. She awoke several hours later and called room service. Once the food arrived, she woke Killa up to eat.

"You play too much," he griped seeing she had pulled his dick out once more. His tune changed when he saw she ordered his favorite blue cheese burger and sweet potato fries. "Thanks."

"You're welcome, Babe," she replied and put a forkful of salad into her mouth.

"That's all you're eating?" he asked in shock. He knew firsthand how she could eat.

"Yeah, or I won't be able to fit into my dress."

As soon as she polished it off, she grabbed the bag from the boutique and retreated into the bathroom. Usually she stripped in front of him and he would turn his head. Not tonight though, she wanted him to see her dressed to kill.

Yolo felt extra girly. After a refreshing shower, she primped and prodded in front of the mirror. The cute, shoulder length blonde wig complimented her bronze skin. Now for the dress, if you could call it that. The spaghetti strapped strip of cloth plunged so low in front it dipped below her navel. She bounced back quite well from childbirth and the ripples of her six-pack were almost back.

Her breasts kept a little of the baby weight and hung plump and heavy. There was no room for panties in the tiny dress so she didn't put any on her freshly shaved kitty cat. She stepped into her high heeled sandals and emerged triumphantly from the bathroom like she had a point to prove.

Actually, she did, and she proved it.

"You ain't cute," Killa frowned looking her up and down, then down and up. It was exactly the reaction she expected.

Yolo

"Thank you!" she cheesed at the clandestine compliment. She tried to bounce but a tittie popped out.

"A-yo, no games. Go murder that bitch and get back," Killa stood and directed forcefully.

"Ok, Daddy," she smiled. On a whim, she crossed the room and hugged him. She felt kind of silly feeling him tense from the display of affection.

She was about to release him and run until he put his arms around her and hugged her back. Yolo cheesed so hard the corners of her mouth touched her ears. She decided to quit while she was ahead and rushed from the room. Her tittie popped out again but she waited until she was in the hall to put it back.

****

"Mmph!" the bouncer exclaimed when Yolo sashayed up to the Pink Palace. Yolo had to squint to verify that he was in fact a she. Standing six feet with long dread locks made it hard to tell.

"I guess that's a compliment," Yolo said feeling sassy. It doesn't matter if you're gay or straight, new meat is new meat. All eyes were on Yolo as she traipsed inside.

"Who the hell is that?" Lil Man demanded with one of those 'Dayum she fine' grimaces on her face. The stud stood the same 5'5" as Yolo with delicate features. No matter how hard she tried not to be, she was still pretty.

Lil Man would ace bandage her breasts and spoke in a husky whisper that left her voice sore. At 25 years old, she had never been with a man and had a brand new vagina in her boxer shorts.

"Cola," Yolo requested as she reached the bar. Lil Man appeared by her side before she could take her first sip.

"Nuh uh lil' mama," she said taking the glass out of Yolo's hand before she could get it up to her mouth. "A bitch like you 'posed to be sippin' bubbly in the VIP, ya heard?"

"Heard you call me a bitch," Yolo replied twisting her lips at the twisted so-called compliment. She drifted away and wondered if the mothers of the civil rights movement referred to themselves or each other as bad bitches. What about the mothers of the believers? Mary? I think not.

"Um...hello?" Lil Man asked bringing Yolo back to the present.

"What?" Yolo snapped at being pulled from her thoughts.

"Come hang out with a nigga," she offered.

It suddenly made sense to her. If you consider yourself a nigga then of course you want a bitch. Niggas and bitches, I'm surprised that's not a book title.

"Sip on these grapes," Lil Man urged.

"I don't drink, but...I'll come hang out with you," she replied coyly. Lil Man exaggerated her swag as she led the new meat up to the VIP section.

It took Yolo a few seconds for her eyes to adjust to the dim lights. She would never adjust to the debauchery within. She was not ready. The place was Sodom and Gomorrah lesbian style.

A very young, very light skin girl lay on a table with her legs spread very far apart. She must have been a cheerleader before becoming a tramp. A large stud tongue fucked her until she came. The stud scooted away and watched her squirt.

"Yeah Ox! You don't play with it!" Lil Man cheered giving her a high five.

"That's right!" the stud proclaimed proudly with a wet smile. She wiped the juice away with the back of her hand and called, "Next!"

"My turn!" a petite black girl yelled and took position on the table.

Yolo felt an odd curiosity watching the girl on girl action. Her panties would be wet if she had worn any.

"Shit girl you can stretch out on my table and I'll hook you up, ya heard," Lil Man offered.

"I've never been with a girl. Shoot, I've only been with one guy and only once," Yolo said truthfully.

"Sho-nuff!" Lil Man shouted as the new meat alarm rang in her head. She was going to turn this one out and keep her for herself. She snatched Yolo by the hand and pulled her towards the door.

"Where are we going?" she asked naively.

"To my spot. I'm finna give yo' lil' ass the bizness," the stud assured her. Once they got into her Benz, they shot across town. Yolo stifled a smile at how easy it was to get her alone. She was thinking with her dick even though it was a strap-on.

Sa'id Salaam

Business was obviously good because Lil Man pulled up to an exclusive waterfront loft building. She jumped out of the car, rushed around, and rushed Yolo inside.

A huge four-poster bed dominated the bedroom. The dresser held a collection of strap-on dicks in different shapes, sizes, and colors. Yolo climbed the set of stairs with Lil Man right behind her. Once they were on top, she leaned in under Yolo's tiny skirt.

"Oh my!" Yolo gasped in confusion when she felt the tongue flick on her vagina from behind.

"Arch your back," Lil Man instructed as she lifted Yolo's skirt over her hips.

"Okay," she said and complied. The stud sucked her bald box until it exploded in her mouth. Yolo tried to collapse but Lil Man held her in place. She commenced to toss her salad like a world-class chef.

"Stay...right...there," Lil Man said and jumped down from the bed. She went over to the dresser and selected one of the strap-ons.

"What do you plan on doing with that?" Yolo asked curiously.

"'Bout to fuck that pretty lil' pussy, ya heard!" she answered. It was however, the wrong answer.

"Oh no you're not," Yolo said pulling her dress off despite the rejection.

Lil Man misunderstood and smiled assuming she was playing coy. She wasn't. She just didn't want any blood on the new dress.

270

"Don't make me take it! Had to rape a lil' young hoe last week. Wanna smoke up a nigga weed and think you ain't fuckin'! Shit, I strapped that ass spread eagle and took it!" she laughed.

Joking about a rape to a girl who was almost raped isn't a very good luck. Joking about it to a lunatic is just plain stupid. Yolo looked at the large straps attached to the bedpost and changed her plans. The stud just earned a long, drawn out, brutal murder.

Yolo hopped down off the bed and moved across the room in a flash. She and Lil Man might have been the same size and weight, but that was all. Yolo beat that poor girl half to death. She then pulled her on to the bed and strapped her down. That was bad, but coming to and seeing Yolo, strapping on her largest strap-on was worse.

The 10-inch job was a novelty item that she never used. Until now.

"W, w, w, what are y, you going to d, d, do do with that?" Lil Man asked in a panic.

"G, g, g, gonna get me some p, p, pussy," Yolo laughed and kneeled between her outstretched legs. Lil Man bucked against the straps as Yolo fondled her vagina. The unused box betrayed her and soaked her fingers. Yolo lined the prosthetic penis up between her labia and plunged inside.

"Yeow!" Lil Man howled as her cherry popped. Yolo fumbled around trying to figure out how to get a good stroke going. She got it down and you couldn't tell her nothing.

"Whose pussy is this? Huh?" she giggled and stroked.

"Y, y, yours," Lil Man admitted sounding like a little lady. Yolo cheesed and stroked harder.

"Argh!" she grunted and pretended to bust a nut like a guy would do. Once her make believe spasms subsided she snatched the dildo out just as roughly as she forced it in.

"So, we straight now?" Lil Man petitioned hopefully.

"Well Lil Man…"

"Demetria, my name is Demetria."

"Ok, well Demetria, I'm Yolo," Yolo said pulling the wig off. "So no, we're not straight."

Yolo climbed up to her head and stuck the head of the strap-on in her mouth. She gave it some pretty good head for a stud while Yolo unstrapped it. Then she shoved it down her throat.

"Ugh!" Lil Man gagged as Yolo put her full weight on the dildo. She squirmed and twisted in the fight for her life but lost. Choked to death by a plastic penis. That's a pretty fucked up way to die, ya heard.

It had become a macabre custom to use the dead mob phones to send dead mob member pictures to Big Rock. Tonight was no exception and Yolo pretended to be a high fashion photographer.

"Vogue. More life," she instructed the corpse as she snapped pictures. Lil Man just lay there with eyes wide from the shock of death.

After sending the pictures to Rock, she searched through the stud's phone. With her nosey ass. She hit pay dirt when she came across a text conversation between Lil Man and Big Rock's right hand man, Bull.

"Sho-nuff?" Yolo exclaimed at the developing mutiny. That was her way in. She didn't think Lil Man would mind so she took her car keys. A last minute plot popped in her head so she took the straps off the bed as well.

"Well?" Killa asked as Yolo finally made it back to the room. He was questioning the mission as well as the confusion on her face.

"She's dead, but um..." Yolo paused and frowned as she wrestled with what transpired.

"But what?" he bolted upright getting alarmed.

"But I think... I think I'm a lesbian?"

"Oh, well yeah. I could have told you that," Killa cracked up and laid back down.

"Ha ha, very funny," Yolo laid back down beside him.

Chapter 34

The long ride from New Orleans to Maryland was made in virtual silence. It was a smooth ride in the borrowed 550 Benz thanks to Lil Man. Yolo spent most of the ride staring out the window in deep thought. Big Rock was dying tomorrow, but what about the next tomorrow? Would she be alive to see it? Would he?

Yolo sat mad at the lone tear that escaped and quickly backhanded it away before he could see it. He did see her wipe but pretended not to. He didn't say anything until they reached Baltimore.

"Let's get a good night sleep," he suggested as he pulled into a hotel parking lot. "I'll get at my people in the morning for guns and information."

"Ok," Yolo replied solemnly, keeping her secret to herself. She followed him into the office to get the room. "One bed, king size."

Killa frowned but complied. He had gotten use to the warm body lying next to him. The memory of her killing his son was all that kept him from going inside her. After separate showers, they met up on the large bed. As usual, an awkward silence preceded sleep.

"So... you gonna give me some or I gotta take it?" Yolo asked wickedly.

"You would have to tie me down and take it!" Killa shot back and rolled over.

"Have it your way," The Lovely Little Lunatic giggled.

****

"What the...A-yo, fuck you doing!" Killa protested when he awoke the next morning.

Most mornings he awoke to find Yolo playing with his dick but she went beyond this morning. Way beyond. This morning she strapped him down to the bed by his ankles and wrists. She let him flail away until he understood he wasn't going anywhere.

"Hey sleepyhead," she sang coming out of the bathroom. The wet hair and towel wrapped around her showed she was fresh out of the shower. When she dropped it that didn't need an explanation either. If his dick wasn't already hard, it would have gotten hard because Yolo was fine.

"What are you up to?" he asked as she slinked forward seductively.

"You said I had to take it if I wanted it, so..." she reminded and placed a kiss on his ankle.

She kissed and licked her way slowly up his legs. His rock hard dick throbbed when she took it in her hand. Starting from the bottom, she ran her tongue up the shaft then swirled it around the swollen head.

"Help, rape," Killa whispered.

He knew he had been caught off guard and accepted what was to come. Like a blowjob really needs acceptance. Yolo took him into her mouth and slowly descended. All the way until she gagged then did it again. A few strokes later, she flipped around into the 69 position.

No one was holding a gun to Killa's head so he didn't have to eat her. When he leaned forward and licked her pretty vagina, it was because he wanted to.

"Sss!" Yolo hissed when she felt his tongue flick on her lonely vagina. She tried to engage in a mutual 69 but couldn't take the pleasure. She lay her head on his dick like a long, hard pillow and enjoyed it. Not for very long though because it didn't take very long for her to cum in his mouth.

"Ok, let me up," Killa demanded after she got what sounded like a really, really, good nut.

"Boy I'm just getting started!" she warned. "We both know this is our last day together. May as well go out with a bang."

"Fine," he gave up as she straddled him. They locked eyes as she reached down and wriggled him inside her.

Killa watched her face contort while she sank on his pole. She winced when she took as much as she could then began to rock. She rocked slow and shallow building steam as she went along. Soon she felt him resting on her cervix.

Yolo leaned forward for a kiss and got chumped. Killa turned his face giving her his cheek. She took it and planted kisses all over his face while he moved his head like a baby resisting mashed green peas and carrots.

Finally, he gave up and in and kissed her back. Yolo came instantly when his tongue entered her mouth. The strong convulsions pushed Killa over the edge and he exploded inside her.

"Ok, let me up," he repeated when they caught their breath.

"Not finished yet," she replied and did a 180 on his still hard dick.

Killa didn't complain when she began to ride him backwards. She came again and then rode him sideways. Two hours and multiple orgasms later, she slumped over completely spent.

"Let me up?" he asked hopefully.

"I can't, I'm sorry but I…"

"What, going to kill me?" he asked. He was ready to accept it if it was his fate. Death had always been a big part of his life so he wouldn't bitch up now.

"No silly! You're my baby daddy, I can't kill you," Yolo sang. "I um, I'm sorry for you know…your son. I'm sorry for shooting him. I'm sorry about killing kids and coo… I'm sorry. I had a really fucked up childhood though."

Killa oddly felt a tinge of remorse. Even though the tears were as real as the contrition, he still wanted to kill her.

"We have to finish what we started. We have to kill Rock," Killa pleaded.

"Oh I got that. You just get some rest. I'll call the hotel and tell them to untie you once I'm done," she said getting dressed. "Oh turns out I'm not a lesbian after all! Oh! Oh! Wouldn't it be crazy if I'm pregnant again?"

"Yeah, crazy" he repeated as she walked from the room. The lunatic had gotten away.

Chapter 35

"W, w, we gotta fi, fi, find that bitch! We gotta kill her," Big Rock whined as he paced back and forth in his plush hideout. His wife twisted her face in disgust at the cowardly bitching.

"Well, Bull can handle it," Latrice said remembering how Bull handled those back shots he gave her. Rock was too busy acting like a pussy to get some pussy. Luckily, for her, he brought his bodyguard.

"Look what I found!" Bull announced leading a hooded figure in at gunpoint. He snatched the hood off and there was Yolo. Head bowed in defeat and hands behind her back.

"Sh, shoo, shoo, shoot that bitch!" Rock yelled ducking behind his disgusted wife.

"Do it yourself," Yolo dared lifting her head with an evil snarl on her face.

"I, I, I w, w, will you know!" Rock shouted from behind Latrice.

"Here boss," Bull said holding out his gun.

Rock rushed over, grabbed it, and pulled the trigger, as Yolo coked her head defiantly.

"Click," Yolo tensed bringing her hands around in front of her. The brass knuckles adorning each dainty hand indicated a brutal death.

"Ok bye now," Latrice said as Bull led her from the room. She blew him a kiss that was just as fake as her smile.

Meanwhile Yolo popped her fangs in her mouth. Rock had no intentions on being beaten or bit and took off running. He ran and took a flying leap through the plate glass window. Bull and Latrice had just stepped outside when he landed on his neck with a sickening crunch.

And that was the end of the Black Mob.

****

Yolo planned to call room service from the airport so her boo could be discovered. That would give her several hours head start in case he decided to come after her. She could take the church money and live happily ever after with her twins. Would have if Anna Maria Santana De La Cruz didn't get the rooms mixed up.

The lonely, overweight, fifty year old Honduran immigrant was supposed to clean room 205 but ended up at 502 by mistake. It was her lucky day. She had stepped all the way in the door before noticing the naked man strapped to the bed.

"Adios mio!" she shouted, ready to run for help.

"Wait, wait! No policia," Killa pleaded. He was wanted in several states after all. "Untie me por favor."

"No polica?" she repeated raising a bushy eyebrow and scratching her chin hair. She realized he couldn't call the police either and moved in for a closer inspection. Anna flipped his flaccid penis and asked "No policia?"

"No policia," Killa said sounding like he wanted to cry.

She fondled him with curiosity of a woman who hadn't had any dick in 25 years. That's because, well, she was a women who hadn't had dick in 25 years. That was 200 pounds ago as well. Killa knew there was no sense in wasting time and willed himself to get an erection. "Pantilones."

"Pantilones?" Anna repeated and picked up his pants. She found the condom he had and put it on him. Killa closed his eyes tightly when she pulled off her huge panties and climbed on top of him. "No policia."

"No policia," he agreed as she put him inside of her. The large woman made a moaning sound as she rocked herself to an orgasm. Luckily, she wasn't greedy and settled for one nut. One nut each that is, because Killa got off too.

"No policia," she reminded as she pulled her big ass panties back on her big ass. She released one wrist and rushed from the room.

"Fucking bitch!" Killa called after her and began to free himself. "Got some good pussy though..."

Killa jumped in the shower and spun around and got back out. He caught a cab to the airport and booked the next thing smoking to LA. As fate would have it Yolo had a brief layover in Phoenix, Killa's flight was non-stop. He would make it there before she did and knew exactly where she was going.

****

"Un huh, ok, un huh," Yolo replied to the nurse's last minute instructions before releasing the twins. She caught some of it and would Google the rest. The happy babies made happy noises, which stole her focus. The meter was running in a waiting taxi so she was in a rush. Not to mention, a killer was on her tail. "Ok, un huh."

"Well, ok then. Good luck," the nurse relented and let her go. The babies were a little weird, but healthy. They would be just fine.

"Hello there," Killa greeted when he spotted Yolo emerge from the hospital. The high-powered scope on the high-powered rifle zoomed in on her face.

Yolo couldn't see him but felt his presence. No doubt about, it Killa was near. She stopped in her tracks and scanned her horizon. She settled her gaze on a roof top several blocks away. That's where she would have taken a shot from and that's where Killa was perched. Yolo accepted her fate and lowered her head in submission. The shot was his to take.

Killa held his breath and slowly squeezed the trigger. Movement below caught his eye and he saw his kids.

"Shit!" he fussed and released the pressure on the trigger.

Yolo looked dead into the scope and smiled. "Love you baby daddy," she mouthed and got into the taxi.

He let out a deep sigh and accepted that it was over.

THE END

Yolo